The Catch

Myrna Griffith

The Catch

ISBN: 978-1-945976-36-0

Published by EA Books Publishing a division of
Living Parables of Central Florida, Inc. a 501c3
EABooksPublishing.com

Dedication

"The Catch" is dedicated to my parents, Eleanor and Ernie Griffith, who always championed my creativity in whatever forms I chose to try.

Chapter One

D etective Otto VanHulster stumbled into his bedroom. The rumpled raincoat clutched in his left hand slipped to the floor. A street light outside the window cast an eerie glow on the mirror facing him. Van, as he preferred to be called felt every one of his forty two years and then some. He hoped the ghastly reflection of himself was due to the light and not how he really looked.

The past twenty four hours had been grueling. The investigations were far from over. Two robberies and a missing person, all in the past week, was more action than the sleepy little tourist town's police force had seen in years. The keen intuition he had developed over years of training and work in New York City was not always appreciated there, but Van was working hard to gain their trust.

He was wet and soggy from the icy cold November rain and too exhausted to undress. He fell face down on his unmade bed.

* * * * * * * * *

The telephone rang. At least Van thought it did. It rang again and he rolled over to reach for the receiver. As he picked it up, he looked at the clock on the bureau.

"Son of a bitch," he swore. "It's only a few minutes past midnight. Just two crummy hours of sleep."

He took a deep breath before he answered the phone.

"Yeah," he growled into the receiver. "Whaddaya want?"

Anna Gorham, Van's sixty year old aunt, apologized for waking him.

"Otto," she said. "We have a problem here at the school and I think it might tie in with the case you're working on, so I didn't call the station yet."

Being called Otto did not please him, but he pushed that aside.

"Okay, Anna; it's all right," he said as he stretched his hand up to the old piano light clamped to the headboard and switched it on. "Tell me about it."

Van tucked the receiver between his shoulder and chin and reached down to grab the raincoat off the floor. He fished around in the pockets until he came up with a damp cigarette package. He listened while Anna explained.

"Well, the old furnace quit, so Harold, the custodian ... you remember him, don't you? Oh dear, I'm sorry. Anyway, he went down to check on it and ..."

Van interrupted and with as much patience as he could muster, asked, "Can you please get to the point, Anna? I haven't had much sleep, you know."

The sudden dead quiet on the other end of the line was exactly what he expected. Anna wasn't angry. She was just collecting her thoughts.

God, how he needed a cigarette. He managed to get one out of the pack, then rummaged around on the bedside table, found a match and lit it.

"Harold found a man, almost dead by the cellar door....about an hour ago," Anna continued.

"Ouch," Van yelped as the match singed his finger and thumb. "Dammit!"

"What's the matter?" Anna asked. "Are you hurt?"

"It's nothing." She didn't know he was smoking again and this wasn't the time to break the news. "I just dropped a shoe on my toe. What do you mean almost dead? Don't tell me he's still alive and you haven't called an ambulance!"

"No, Otto. Oh dear, I'm not explaining very well. He must have died just a few minutes after Harold found him. I think he'd been shot. There was blood all over the place."

"For pete's sake, Anna," he said angrily. "Why didn't you call me right away?"

"I did. I didn't know anything about it, myself until I went to find out why Harold was taking so

3

long. I found him sitting on a cellar step, sobbing. Poor Harold. He was so frightened."

Although Harold was a great handyman, Van knew he wasn't blessed with much in the common sense department.

He softened his voice. "Sorry ... go on."

Anna continued. Van crumpled up the unlit cigarette. After wetting his thumb and fingertip to check the match, he tossed them both in the direction of the corner wastebasket. He listened, automatically extracting bits and pieces of information and storing it in his well-trained memory for future use.

When his aunt paused, Van jumped off the bed, the phone still cradled on his shoulder.

"Don't touch, move or disturb anything. You know the drill. I'll call the station and be there in ten minutes!"

He made the call, grabbed the soggy raincoat and dashed out the door.

* * * * * * * * *

On his way to the Harrington Girls' Boarding School, Van imagined the scene awaiting him. Even though his aunt was probably shaken, he was fairly confident that she would be handling the situation in her usual cool, professional manner.

Harold, on the other hand would be a different story. Van pictured him running around, dazed, his bright wiry red hair sticking out all over his head and blood smeared on his hands and clothes. *Good God, he'll scare those teenage girls to death.*

He cursed himself for not asking more questions before he raced out of his apartment. What if Anna was dealing alone with the whole school in an uproar at that very minute? But she didn't sound that flustered on the phone.

Van wanted to fly to his aunt's aid, but he did his best to stay close to the speed limit in his thickly settled neighborhood. As soon as he came to open road, he slammed his foot down on the gas pedal. The surge of speed and the roar of the restored 1966 engine in his red MG gave him a sense of power. False as it might be, it always made him feel a little more in control.

Maybe he'd be lucky. Van forced himself off the worry and on to the work ahead. If Anna was able to stay calm and take charge in time, then the little lambs would all be tucked into their beds where they belonged.

He tried to envision the cellar door of the old school. It was on the left side of the main building in the very back corner. Many years had passed since Van roamed those grounds as a young boy visiting his aunt, but he remembered the vine covered cellar steps were almost concealed from view until you were standing right in front of them.

It had been the perfect hiding place for him when he was playing. Now it was a gruesome one. A dying man had found it. Or had someone brought him there?

As Van turned the MG into the circular drive in front of the school, he checked his watch. Eleven minutes. Well, he was close. Anna would not take his ten-minute promise seriously anyway.

For some reason the words 'white horse' had been echoing all week, over and over in his mind. They dogged him, badgered him, demanding answers he wasn't yet able to provide. Pieces of a puzzle he was anxious to put together. Why were they playing in his head now? Was this death connected to the other crimes?

The torrents of rain that had plagued him the day before, making his investigations a soggy affair, had changed into a fine mist. Van parked near the front steps. He snaked his six foot, three inch frame up and out of the tiny car. His eyes made a sweep of the surrounding area as he stuffed himself back into the still damp and wrinkled raincoat.

Everything looked quiet. In the light from the two Victorian lanterns framing the walk up to the entrance to the brick building, the lush grass gleamed and sparkled in the light breeze. The cement walkway was long and wide enough for a horse and carriage to maneuver the discreet dropping off and picking up of guests back in the days when Harrington House had been an Inn for the wealthy. Two huge horse chestnut trees, perfectly centered, graced each side of the front lawn.

Van walked quickly through the side yard, thinking he was alone. Then he noticed a small group of girls milling around near a classroom doorway. He had forgotten that an addition had been added recently. It made the trip around to the back a lot longer than he'd planned.

Van strained his ears, expecting to hear at least a little commotion, which might lead him to where he was needed most.

There was nothing. Why weren't those girls talking amongst themselves, trying to stifle an occasional nervous giggle? His puzzlement deepened when he noticed they were not in pajamas, but in casual daytime clothes. All of them. What were they doing out there that late at night?

The hair on the back of Van's neck stood at attention. Somehow he knew it wasn't from the cold air. *This whole scene gives me the willys.*

Rather than continue to the cellar door, he headed back to the front entrance and found Anna waiting there. The two spotlights over the door framed her and made her look as if she was on stage. The statuesque sixty year old manager of Harrington Boarding School was bundled up in a man's dark double-breasted sailor-type pea jacket.

Below the jacket, a red and black plaid robe fluttered around her legs. Her long white and wheat colored hair, loosely braided, rested gently over one shoulder.

When they were close enough to each other, Anna gave him a quick hug and pushed the top of his unbuttoned coat aside. She slipped a small key into his shirt pocket. "Lordy, you are soaked, my pet."

"What's that?" he asked.

"Later," she whispered. "Not here."

Out loud, Anna said, "It's a good thing most of the girls are still away for the holiday."

Van started to ask about the girls in the yard, but she was ready for him. It was uncanny the way she was always able to tune in and seem to know what he was thinking.

"That group around the corner of the building has just come back from a day in Corinth. The cook and his wife felt sorry for the girls who had nowhere to go for Thanksgiving, so they piled them into the van and left them off at the mall while they did our grocery shopping."

"But, it's very late," he protested. "Why are they still up?"

Anna answered quickly, but Van noticed a little edge to her voice. "Apparently, they talked the two softies into a movie. I was worried sick. Won't let that happen again."

It wasn't that he didn't believe her story, but she seemed different; maybe more nervous and cautious, as if she were weighing her words.

Yeah, the story fit, but Van's aunt had never been what you'd call flexible about rules and regulations. It seemed strange that she hadn't sent the girls right to their rooms.

He sighed and gave Anna a reassuring pat on the hand.

"Everything's going to be all right. Why don't you go back up to your apartment? And let's get those girls to the dorm where they belong, too."

He watched her face, looking for clues to her thoughts. She definitely seemed different. *She's holding something back, that's for sure.*

Exasperated, he added sarcastically, "I don't need them underfoot!"

Anna grimaced and nodded. "I know Otto, you're right. I don't mean to make your job more difficult." She hurried off to find and collect the girls.

Van couldn't waste any more time. He snapped into detective mode. *Jeez----what the hell is wrong with me? I should have gone straight to that damn cellarway.*

The dead man was the most important thing to deal with. Why had he let himself be thrown off the track by those students? Befuddled, he scratched his head and broke into a trot around the opposite side of the building to the back of the school. With the help of the front lamps and spotlights, Van scooted, dodging the many trees and bushes, just as he had done when he was a youngster. He stopped at the corner of the brick section to reset his bearings when he found no light to guide him to the cellar door.

Just as he was wondering what was taking the ambulance and police so long, a sweep of bright lights from an approaching squad car streaked across the side yard. He turned and as the first vehicle slowed, the headlights swept by a large oak tree not more than twenty feet away from him. He thought he was hallucinating when he caught sight of a young female figure leaning against the tree trunk. He took a couple of quick steps back into the dark behind a rose bush to his right. From there he was able to see her more clearly.

The girl seemed motionless. At first, he thought she might be in shock. Then, her right hand moved to brush a lock of hair away from her eyes. An eerie, twisted smile washed over her face. Then slowly, as if melting, she disappeared behind the tree.

Chapter Two

The girl must have felt him watching her. She ran into the dorm building. Van started to go after her, but was interrupted by one of the police officers.

"Hey, Van—what the hell's going on here? What are you doing behind this bush? Or shouldn't I ask?"

"Oh, Hi Brad. Ho, ho, very funny. Come around to the back of the building with me. There's a dead guy in the cellar-way."

"Okay, right," Brad responded, then shouted to two other officers standing by the squad car. "C'mon—bring a light. Hurry up!"

Brad pointed his own flashlight as Van used his hands to separate the heavy thicket of ivy nearly obscuring the pathway. He stopped each time he swiped a clump of it aside and held it so the others could do the same. He hoped the left side of the building had not been enlarged and that the route would be shorter.

"Jeez, Van, you sure know your way around here. How come?" Brad asked.

"Used to play all over these grounds when I visited my aunt as a kid. Here it is."

The width of the cellar stairs would only allow one adult person at a time, so Van stepped gingerly down the four slimy moss covered steps. There was about two inches of rain water in the stairwell. The dead man was in a sitting position at the bottom of the stairs. One leg was sprawled across the landing, the other bent sideways at an awkward angle and leaning up against the wall.

"Gimme that lamp and pass me some gloves," Van ordered. "Lotsa blood here."

Once Van had the gloves on, he reported to Brad, "Doesn't look like more than one gunshot wound, but I see more blood near his abdomen.. He's been badly beaten and his right leg looks broken, too. Poor guy must have bled to death down here after somebody dumped him. Son of a bitch—when is that freakin' ambulance gonna get here?"

Just as he spoke the words, he heard the wail of a siren coming closer and closer to the school. He muttered, "What the hell, the guy's dead anyway. Did anyone call the coroner?"

Brad answered. "Gina's on her way, Van. Gotta drive all the way from Newcastle, though. She's not on call, but we couldn't find Larry. You and Larry are going to owe her, big time."

"Great, just what I need." Gina Taylor's grating personality and arrogant attitude was something that Van had trouble tolerating in general; he really hated to work closely with her.

"That's probably her coming now, then. I can hardly wait. "Hey", Van growled then raised his voice. "Can one of you guys squeeze down a couple of stairs and hold a light for me? Don't forget gloves though, or Gina will go spastic."

Not only was it hard for Van to move around in the cramped space, but there was so much blood everywhere that he hardly dared to touch the body for fear of making Gina's job more difficult.

Once Van had both hands free and more light, it was easier to check out the man's face. His eyes were open. Fear seemed locked into them. His mouth was stretched wide open and full of blood. He looked to be in his late fifties. Deep creases and heavily tanned skin suggested he had worked most of his life outdoors. Maybe a fisherman. Van was able to reach into one of the man's jacket pockets and found a matchbook. There it was again. 'White Horse Inn'. Those words, the ones that badgered him, the ones he couldn't get out of his mind.

He called up to the officers, "One of you guys should go find the janitor, Harold. See what he has to say and keep him available. I'll need to talk to him, too, but keep him away from here."

A familiar voice cut through the darkness. It was Gina. "I need a machete for this damn jungle. Somebody shine a damn light so I can see where to go for chrissake!!"

Brad inched back up the steps and waved his flashlight in her direction.

Gina arrived, her own light weaving back and forth, a loud growling sound coming from her mouth.

"Okay—show me," she demanded.

Van backed himself carefully up the steps and jumped out of the way so she could get down to examine the body. He didn't bother to warn her that it was slippery. "Want me to get the EMT's over here now?"

"Nahhhh, not until I figure out how I want him moved."

Van and Brad stood at the top of the steps, patiently waiting for her orders.

"Damn—so much blood from one vic. All right, get the crew," she bellowed. "And a hoist. We'll have to lift him out, straight up."

Van gave Brad's arm a light punch. "I'll go. I can find my way without a light. You stay here."

"Oh, yeah, sure, Van. Thanks a lot. You're a real pal."

Chapter Three

A t two A.M., Van sat in his aunt's den. From his seat on the blue chintz covered couch, he heard the familiar clatter of dishes and the sound of tap water streaming into a kettle.

When he was working in his hectic, coffee-dependent occupation, he never considered drinking tea. Funny how his habits automatically changed when he stepped into Anna's world; though he would prefer coffee.

As far as Van could tell their relationship was unique. None of his friends claimed to have an older woman in their lives that they could really trust. And wives and girl friends were definitely kept in the dark about what their police work entailed. Some preferred it that way, so as not to worry so much, but Van was disappointed to find that in some cases, it was the man who had reasons to hide things.

Anna and Van were very close. As far back as he could remember, he had spent more time with her than either of his parents.

Van didn't want to alter Anna's tea routine. Better to keep her as relaxed as possible. His intent was to make her feel comfortable enough to tell him what was going on at the school.

Anna came into the room balancing a large plate. On it were two Dagwood size sandwiches. "I won't ask you when you ate last. Just be a good boy and eat these. I promise I'll not force dessert on you," she said as she plunked the plate down on the ceramic topped coffee table in front of him. "Be right back with the tea."

Van snatched up one of the sandwiches. His aunt's order would cause no problem. Come to think of it, he wasn't really sure when or what he'd eaten last.

Most of the first sandwich was gone when Anna came in with the steaming teapot in one hand and two china mugs clutched with the thumb and forefinger of the other.

He laughed as she placed them carefully on the table. "Anna, you never cease to amaze me."

As Anna poured, Van gobbled up the rest of the sandwich and started to reach for the second one. He changed his mind. This was not one of their casual visits. Not like those glorious good old days when he was young and innocent and his parents left him with Anna when they went abroad.

Anna was his dad's sister, had been married once, but was widowed at a very young age and had no children of her own. The girls at Harrington became her children and Van was pretty confident he was her special nephew.

Memories can be lovely, but the reason he was there was more important than those or his appetite. He leaned back on the couch and reached into his shirt pocket. "Okay, Anna—what's with this key?"

At first, she ignored the question and finished pouring tea into their cups. She sighed and then settled into the green upholstered chair next to the couch.

"Well, Otto, I'm not sure. I found it on the top step of the cellar stairs. It's nothing like the keys we use here."

Van turned the key from one side to the other. "It looks fairly new. Kinda like a locker key. I'll take it downtown. My guys can check the bus terminal and train station."

Van was finding his usual effortless concentration on facts difficult to summon up. "Oh yeah - - and the airport, too."

For some reason, the strange atmosphere of the murder scene haunted him; especially that girl by the tree.

"Anna, did you notice anything unusual about your girls tonight? I mean, they seemed a lot more subdued than I expected. Had you read them the riot act or something before I got here?"

Again, she didn't answer right away, but picked up her cup and started to drink her tea. That was out of character. His aunt was more often way ahead of him, anticipating questions before he posed them and quick with her responses.

Van prodded, "C'mon now Anna. There's something going on here, isn't there? This isn't like you to hold anything back from me."

"I know, Otto. It's got me stymied. Maybe I'm losing my knack for picking up on things like I used to. Old age is creeping in, you know."

Van shook his head. "No way, no how, lady," he protested. "I'm not sure my feelings are worth a tinker's dam either at this point, so don't go putting yourself down."

"Thank you, dear. Nice of you," she said and continued. "Well, I have noticed that the girls do seem to have lost some of their usual exuberance, but I just noticed it last week and chalked it up to the holiday blues."

Van reached for his cup and took a sip. "When did you first think there was a change?"

A puzzled expression wrinkled Anna's brow. "That's hard to say. I guess it's been a gradual thing. So subtle I didn't realize it was happening. Why do you ask?"

"That girl." Van clicked into his serious detective mode.

"That girl, the one I saw under the tree." The information gathering questions formed rapidly into their well-learned sequence.

"Did you see her? Who is she? I didn't get a good look at her."

"Oh, Otto, I'm not sure," Anna trembled and put her cup down with a clatter. "I do remember seeing Kathleen Sullivan out in the driveway earlier, while the others were gone. But it was hours before we discovered that man."

Van prodded. "Tell me about her. Everything, anything. And why didn't she go with the others today?"

Anna was visibly rattled. He'd struck a nerve; that was plain to see. Why was she holding back? Where was that familiar no-holds-barred stream of discussion? Could his rock solid aunt be afraid?

Van leaned forward and placed one hand on her shoulder. He spoke in the soft practiced tone that was known to make even jumpy murder suspects trust him. "Now Anna, I know this is hard for you. I don't know why, but we'll figure it out. Just take your time and start from the first time you noticed anything. Doesn't matter if it didn't seem important then. Just think about what happened to make you think twice about it, okay?"

Anna told him that Kathleen had only been with them for three weeks. She seemed like a very bright girl, good grades and all.

Then Anna's eyes lit up. "That's it. That's when it all started. Oh Otto, I think we're getting somewhere!"

"Great. Keep going. What happened? Don't stop now." Van's patience was wearing thin. His lack of sleep didn't help the matter much. "Anna, I have to be back to work in four hours. Please help me out, here."

Anna took a quick sip of tea, cleared her throat and continued. "There was one day, about a week ago. It was an exam day and the girls were all nervous, of course. But, it seemed like a different kind of nervous. There was a lot of bickering going on and a couple of girls got into a fist fight. Fortunately, I was near enough to intervene."

"Was this girl, Kathleen involved in the fight?" Van asked, the eerie expression on the girl's face clear in his mind.

"Not directly, she wasn't. But, I remember she was there. Come to think of it, she was egging one of the girls on. Funny, I didn't think that was significant at the time. Do you think it was?"

Van wasn't sure yet what any of it meant. He thought it would be a good idea to keep an eye on Kathleen, so he asked Anna to do that as well as she could.

"I can't explain, but I can't get her out of my head. You should have seen the weird look on her face tonight. Almost like she was enjoying some private joke. "

Anna was back in action. "What else do you want to know? I can go get her file right now if you want."

"Oh, no, but I would like to know more, like what the fight was about. I'll call you from the station tomor—err, I mean today. Say around one o'clock?"

All of a sudden, Van's adrenaline gauge needle came to a halt on empty. He looked at his watch: three thirty A.M. "Whew, I gotta get some shut-eye. If I crash here on the couch, can you make sure I get up at six?"

Anna nodded her head. "I'll get you a pillow and blanket and I'll give you my alarm clock."

By the time Anna did up the dishes, Otto was sound asleep on the couch. It was four A.M. and she was exhausted, too. She skipped her usual neat kitchen clean up ritual and left the dishes to dry in the drainer.

On the way to her bedroom, Anna lifted the calendar from its hook over the hallway telephone table. It still bothered her that she had taken so long to notice a difference in the girls' behavior and she hoped the calendar would help remind her of any events that would provide clues. Armed with a pen, a pad of paper and the calendar, she climbed into bed. She was prepared, yes, but didn't have a whole lot of confidence in herself. It's been a long time since *I've helped Otto on a case. Not sure the detective in me is working like my younger days.*

She laid her weary head on the pillow and closed her eyes. After a few minutes, she remembered Van's comments about Kathleen. She turned the calendar page back to October and circled the date the girl had arrived from New York City.

Chapter 4

When Anna woke, she instinctively grabbed for the items that were in her hands last, but found nothing. She reached to turn the bedside lamp off, only to find that there was still light in her room. It was the sunshine. She lifted her arm to check her watch.

"I put them on the bureau." The male voice startled her. Van stepped into her room.. "It's almost ten thirty."

"Otto, what are you still doing here? Didn't the alarm clock work? Oh my God ... I should be in my office by now."

"Don't worry. It worked. I've already been downtown." Van had decided to come back and check on her before he went home to try to get a few hours of sleep.

"I hope I did the tea right. If you dare take a chance, I'll bring you some."

Anna sniffed the air. "It doesn't smell like you burned anything so I'll try it. But then I have to get going."

Van grinned, rubbed his hands together like a mad scientist and hurried off to the kitchen.

Anna chuckled as a memory of Otto as a young boy drifted back to her. The occasion was her birthday and he begged her to stay in bed so he could serve breakfast in bed like the big people did. It seemed like yesterday, but was at least twenty-five years ago. *I'll never forget that sparkle in his eyes, she thought.*

There was still a little bit of that sparkle left from time to time, but now there was much more to read in those eyes. Her special nephew had grown into a sincere and compassionate man. It was her turn to be proud.

Anna had found it difficult, at first, to accept his choice of the police academy over college, but soon realized that it was foolish to waste time worrying.

The tray Van set down on her lap was impressive. Instead of a simple cup of tea, her favorite Royal Vinton green 'willow" plate was barely visible under a huge mound of fluffy scrambled eggs. Four perfectly positioned toast points rested precariously on the edge of the plate.

"My goodness, you've been busy. This is wonderful. Way too much, but wonderful. Now why don't you get youself a fork and help me eat this."

Van smiled, reached into his back pocket and produced a fork. "I was hoping you'd say that."

He dragged a chair up to the side of the bed and pulled a napkin out of his shirtsleeve. "My plate is under yours."

Anna scraped more than half of the eggs onto Van's plate. He didn't protest.

Just as he started to take his first mouthful, Anna's phone rang.

"Don't move," he said. "It's probably for me anyway." He rushed into the living room to answer it.

"Yeah … no kidding." It was obvious he was talking loudly for her benefit, so she didn't feel guilty listening in. "Which station, bus? … train? … or airport?"

A couple of minutes passed with Van just listening, then he spoke. "The airport is only twenty minutes from here. Makes sense, Jimbo. Oh sure, I'm fine. Course I'll make it. Yeah, right pal. I may be older, but I can still beat the pants off of you on the squash court."

Jimbo's real name was James Kenton Reilly. He and Otto had grown up in the same neighborhood in Brooklyn, New York and in spite of the four years gap in age and differing financial backgrounds, they grew to be inseparable buddies. Now, as grown men, they seemed to compete with each other with a fierceness that belied their deep friendship. Anna didn't understand it, but thought perhaps it was a cover to keep the rest of the police force from knowing how close they really were. At any rate, knowing that Jim was Otto's partner against crime somehow made her worry less.

Otto hung up the phone and ambled back into the bedroom. "Jim says 'hi' and his wife invited us over to supper sometime. Seems the twins ask about you all the time. Guess you made a hit with them at the last family cookout."

Otto's expression had changed. Anna knew his mind was elsewhere.

"I recognize that look. You have to get going, right?"

"You guessed it. Meeting Jim for coffee." He grabbed two heaping mouthfuls of the egg.

"I know. The dynamic duo is off and running again."

He winked at her and gave her a quick hug. "Right again, Detective Gorham," he teased. "You get some rest. Your office can do without you this morning. We may need you later."

* * * * * * * * *

Van met Jim at the coffee shop near the station. He had good news. Forensics had worked fast. Once the dead man's fingerprints were not found on the key, getting the court order to open the airport locker had been a cinch. The information was then quickly released back to Van to speed up the investigation.

"Guess I'll have to cut Gina some slack for a while," Van admitted. "She did a great job this time."

The Baseford Airport was only ten minutes from the police station, but this was a Monday morning and traffic in the small town was at the mercy of cautious, lumbering school busses.

Van was happy he had asked Jim to drive. He knew he wouldn't have his partner's patience and he needed time to concentrate on the details he recently learned from Phil.

The 'White Horse Inn' connection wasn't clear yet, but he ran it by Jim anyway.

"You've lived here longer than me, Jimbo. Do you remember anything about the woman who died there?"

Jim just shook his head. "That was all taken care of by the Corinth guys and they didn't want us to ask questions. Pretty much told us to 'butt out'."

It was eleven thirty in the morning when Van and Jim got to the airport.

Van was still deep in thought when they entered the lobby. They'd only gone a few steps when Jim stopped him.

"Hold it," Jim said as he flashed his arm out sideways to stop Van from walking any farther. "Check out the dame by the lockers"

Van bobbed his head to see around a group of senior citizens zig-zagging through the small

LaRoque County Airport. He pulled Jim over to the bank of pay phones and sat down on one of the stools.

"I'm going to stay here and fake a phone call and talk loud enough to hopefully distract her. Here's the key. Number fifty two, I think. You do the look-see."

The two men had played a similar scene many times. Jim alternately checked his watch, looked at the arrival and departure schedule over the ticket counter and then scanned the lobby.

Once the area cleared out a bit, Van had a better view of the woman from where he sat. She was tall and willowy Her short shiny brown hair glimmered with every move she made. *Looks like a wig, to me.* Her handbag, strapped crisscross over her torso looked large enough to be an overnighter.

Van spoke softly into the tiny radio clipped to the inside of his raincoat lapel. "What's she doing, Jimbo?"

Jim pulled a white handkerchief out of his pants pocket and wiped his nose while leaning his head closer to the radio attached to his belt. "Looks like she's trying to pry open a locker with a nail file or something. Number might be in the fifties, too. She sure is nervous; keeps looking over her shoulder. Think we should stop her?"

Van stood up, grabbed a phone receiver and shook his head, vehemently. He yelled into the receiver loud enough for Jim to hear. "No, honey ... I told you ... I can't get there in time. You'll just have to wait, dammit!"

The ploy worked. Along with many others, the woman turned to see what was happening. Van got a full view of her.

Wow, what a looker. Her face looked like a professional had made her up. *Maybe she's a dancer or an actress.*

He looked around, pretending to seem apologetic to the onlookers. Once he felt the attention was not on him anymore, he lowered his voice again and talked to Jim.

"No, let's get a closer look, first." He pointed to the coffee shop about ten feet from where the woman stood. "Go order a couple of coffees and I'll be right over."

By the time Van joined Jim the woman had given up trying to get the lock open and had walked over to the waiting area. She sat down next to an older woman who was wearing a kerchief and sunglasses. They carried on a short, but animated conversation, then collected their scattered belongings.

The younger woman had a small expensive looking suitcase. The older one only carried a large purse and a small cosmetic case.

When they seemed ready to leave, Van decided to send Jim to tail them. "I'll call Kevin to meet us here. If you can keep them in your sights, we'll have him take over. I want to get that locker open."

"Righto, Boss." Jim made a mock salute, clicked his heels and dashed for the revolving door.

He got there just in time to offer his assistance. He bowed gallantly to the women juggling their bags while trying to get through the door.

Van watched, chuckling. *That Jim is such a ham. He should be an actor. But then, what would I do without him?*

He took his coffee and returned to a phone booth. Turning his back to the few people milling around, he unclipped his radio and used it to call headquarters. That done, he turned, took a big gulp of the bitter brew Jim had bought for him and made a disgusting face. He walked, deliberately over to a trash barrel. With the meanest look he could muster, he snapped the cover back on and threw it away.

I hate to act mean and nasty, but I hope it keeps folks away. Don't want any questions to slow me down.

Van left the airport terminal to join his partner outside. He caught sight of him as soon as he stepped out. Jim, about thirty feet to Van's left was walking backward toward the parking lot. He signaled with a quick wave. It was safe to follow.

Van glanced around to see if he was attracting any unwanted attention and found the few people outside to be moving along to their own destinations. No one stopped to gawk at him. He broke into a purposely designed semi trot that looked more like a traveler's fast walk than a policeman's run.

He caught up to Jim. "Where'd they go, pal?"

Jim pointed to a taxi pulling out of the parking lot. "Don't worry. I know the driver and here's his plate number." He handed Van a wrinkled gum wrapper.

"It's all I had, buddy."

Van was in motion before Jim finished talking. "C'mon. We'll radio Kev so he can take over the surveillance. I want to get into that locker."

Chapter 5

J im, surgical gloves on his hands, tried to open the number fifty two airport locker. "This key's a little beat up. Doesn't seem to want to go in all the way. Are you sure that dame was this far down to the right? I thought it was more like in the middle."

"Well, maybe so," Van replied. "But keep trying, okay? Remember, she was fiddling with the lock when we came in. Could be she messed it up a little."

Van checked his watch. It had only been a few minutes since Kevin had started tailing the two women, but Van was anxious. He wanted to call the station, but he didn't want Jim to know how perplexed he was yet. At least not until he could fit together some more of the puzzle pieces.

I'm still wondering how to explain why the face of a young boarding school student is still haunting me. So far, he had nothing to back up his gut feeling that she knew something about the murder.

"Hey," Jim said as the locker door sprung open. "I got it. Hope it's the right one, Boss."

Van was too curious to waste time on a clever comeback. He struggled to stretch tight surgical gloves over his long fingers. He pulled a large folded plastic evidence bag out of his coat pocket and snapped it open.

Jim stepped aside. "Doesn't look like much, does it?"

Van felt a tingle at the base of his neck, just like he'd felt the night before at the school. "We'll see. Never can tell."

The items in the locker did seem pretty ordinary. He carefully pulled out a badly wrinkled and dingy men's white shirt, checked the one pocket and found nothing but small pieces of stale tobacco.

Van sniffed at the shirt material then handed the shirt to Jim. "Looks like our guy was a smoker, Jimbo."

"Yeah, Forensic might be able to do something with that tobacco, right?"

It was the type of question Jim asked quite often of his partner. He seemed ever curious and eager to learn all he could about the forensic side of law enforcement. He had expressed interest in taking some classes, but, so far was busy supporting a wife and three kids. Van knew this and so was very willing to share anything he had learned about it.

Jim fished a plastic bag out of his jacket pocket, took the shirt and folded it carefully so the tobacco would not fall out, then put the whole shirt into the gallon size bag.

Next, Van found a pair of men's pants. He handed them to Jim. "You check these. Separate bag, please. There's a package or something in the back, here."

Van knew that Jim was always happy to be an active part in investigations, but he was expecting a jibe.

It came. "Oh sure ... you get to do all the fun stuff, right?"

Van smiled. "Of course. What did you expect?"

He reached over the few small items in the locker and wrapped his hand around a small parcel. Something snapped.

""Shit ... the thing bit me," he snarled when his hand hit the top of the locker. He drew it out fast.

Jim peered inside the locker and laughed. "It's only a rubber band. Probably broke when you touched it. Boy.....you're damn jumpy, Van."

Van glared at his partner and friend. "Yeah, what of it?"

There was a short blast of silence between them, then Jim answered. "Hey, hey, hey. Sorry Pal. Just picking on you like always. Jeez, I didn't mean anything by it."

Van took a breath and started to apologize, but he stopped when he saw a small green object fall out of the pants Jim was holding. He bent down to get a closer look.

"What's this," he asked as he swiped a gentle karate chop to Jim's kneecap. "Looks like a matchbook."

Van picked it up. It was mangled and felt damp. One side was just a plain color green, but the other side had printing. His stomach did a flip-flop. *White Horse Inn.* There it was again. The odd sense of familiarity washed over him. The neck tingle returned and kept traveling down his spine. The address was worn away, but there was a telephone number. He showed it to Jim.

"Ever hear of this place, Buddy?"

"No. Can't recall anything like it around here. If the inn had a restaurant, though, Ginny and I would have tried it by now." Jim handed the pants back to Van and took a notepad and pencil out of his jacket pocket. "See. I'm prepared this time."

"Congratulations. Whatcha gonna write?"

"Well, I'm not too great about remembering the names of places we go, but Ginny's a whiz." He wrote down the name and number. "Could probably even tell you what their specials are, too. I'll run it by her if that's okay."

"Sure, sure. That would be great. I know you won't tell her anything that would mess up the investigation. "She's true-blue." *And you're a lucky shit to have her,* Van thought.

Van studied the phone number. It was not a local exchange and wasn't any he recognized either. "Five-one-eight-four-three-six-five-zero-five-zero; got it? There've got to be some answers waiting wherever this joint is."

He popped the matches back into the pants pocket and checked the other pockets. He found nothing except a soiled white handkerchief. Jim put them into a clear trash-size plastic bag.

Van reached gingerly into the locker again and carefully scooped the package toward him. It looked harmless enough, but one could never tell. "May be a packet of mail. That might be helpful. Got another bag on ya?"

Jim nodded and transferred the pack into a clean bag.

The remaining items in the locker didn't produce any surprises. A couple of wedding bands in a small box, a ladies watch and an old pearl necklace didn't seem like much, but on closer examination might give up some clues. He was ready to hand the locker dusting over to Gina's team.

Van was disappointed. He wondered if all detectives experienced the same initial rush of excitement when clues surfaced and then the huge let down when nothing major was uncovered right away.

Jim must have been either thinking the same or reading Van's mind. "Well, this isn't a lost cause yet. I can't wait to see what's in that bundle."

Van looked around the airport lobby. A small number of curious travelers and workers had gathered not far from them. Neither of the women suspects were present.

"Yeah, let's scram. Lock her back up, Jimbo. Too many gawkers here."

"You drive," Van announced when they reached the squad car. I want to check this wad of mail or whatever it is."

"No problem," Jim responded. "I figured that's why you kept the "surgies" on. And, of course ... you get all the fun again."

Chapter 6

B ack at headquarters that afternoon, Van sat in his tiny cramped office. The main section of the station was already at maximum capacity when he arrived from New York two years ago. His childhood friend, Jim had talked him into applying for the detective position which the chief wasn't convinced the small town of Harrington needed. For the first few weeks, Van had shared Jim's desk.

Eventually, Chief Stan Rocket accepted the change and the utility room at the back of the workspace was emptied. That

became Van's office.

Van's desk was covered with letters taken from the locker. All the same size and mostly written on light weight air mail paper. They seemed to all be penned by the same person and the post marks read New York City.

"Somehow, I knew it would be a woman ... well, female anyway. It's hard to tell what her age is. What do you guess, Jimbo?"

Jim, perched on a high stool in the corner, reached for one of the letters. "Young, that's for sure. Maybe early twenties, but no more than that.

She sounds like she knows her way around out there in the jungle, too."

"By jungle, I'm guessing you mean our NYC, right?"

Jim nodded. "Yep. Sounds to me like she grew up in a neighborhood even tougher than ours. Probably had no choice but to learn street smarts the hard way."

Jim reminded Van that he had worked a couple of years on the police force in Greenwich Village. "Two years was enough for me. I don't know how some of those kids survive."

"I know," Van reflected. "I don't know how I lasted as long as I did on the city force either. You didn't have any kids of your own then, did you?"

"No, but as soon as we learned Ginny was pregnant, I decided to get out. I didn't want any of my kids growing up in that environment. I think she was relieved,"

"Yeah, you got yourself an angel there, buddy. She probably would have stayed there if she thought it would make you happy."

Van sighed. It sure would be nice to have a wife like Ginny.

Geez, I must be wiped out, otherwise I wouldn't be letting myself think about her. Sheila, Sheila … how he missed that woman. It had been a year and three months since she had left him and gone to Scotland. He wondered how many souls she'd led to the Lord by now.

Yes, that was a snide thought, but he couldn't help it. He was jealous of those people. It was a very wonderful thing she was doing. He wished he could be as sure of his life's goals as Sheila was of hers.

"So, have you heard from her lately?" Jim asked.

Van broke free of his inner thoughts and laughed. "Damn, you know me too well, Jimbo."

"Was I right? You started thinking about her when my angel popped into your mind."

Van nodded. "Right as rain. I wonder if I'll ever get her out of my system. I still can't get through a whole week without thinking about her."

Before Jim could break in, Van continued. "Now, don't bug me to call her. I tried that; it just makes it worse."

"Okay, okay." Jim threw his hands up in the air. "'Nuff said. Let's get back to this homicide. Makes for better conversation, anyway!"

"Yeah, you're right, man. Back to the old grind."

Van picked up a letter. He repeated the fact that all were postmarked NYC. He asked Jim to call the post office to find out which part of New York City it was.

Jim reached for the phone on Van's desk. Van stopped him. "No. Could you use another phone? I have to make a call, myself"

"Hey, whatever. You're the boss." Jim winked and added, "Sometimes. Okay if I look at a couple more letters first, though?"

"Yeah, sure, but make sure that address info is on my desk before you go home tonight."

Van and Jim opened and read a few more letters. They were signed with love, but so far there was no proof of a family connection. It seemed to Van that they were written to either a child or young person, possibly from an aunt, but they lacked any sentimentality or closeness. Most read like a diary of daily activities.

Jim had one letter in his hand. "Hey, this one feels heavy. Might be something in it."

Van reminded him, "Be careful with it. Don't let anything drop on the floor."

Jim was already leaning toward the center of the desk. Van cleared a space.

There was, indeed something besides a letter in the envelope. Out slid a small shiny gold object.

"Looks like a piece of jewelry", Van said as he picked it up. "But it's not a whole piece. What do you think, Jimbo?" He handed the object to Jim.

"Looks like a catch."

"What's a catch, Van asked.?

"You know, the part on a necklace or bracelet that holds it together.

"Oh, you mean a clasp?"

Jim laughed. "Okay. Catch is what I call it, your high-falutin' friends might prefer, 'clasp'."

Van made a swipe for Jim's shoulder, but his partner was too fast for him. He ducked back out of the way.

"Hah…..I saw that comin."

Van looked more closely at the catch. There were small links of chain attached. He dug a long handled magnifying glass out of his desk drawer and found the last link bent out of shape. "I think this was ripped off of someone's neck."

He passed it and the glass to Jim to see.

Jim nodded. "Sure does look that way, Boss. Wonder if it means anything, though."

"Let's both read the letter and see if she mentions it," said Van.

A few minutes later, they both agreed that there was nothing mentioned in that letter that explained the 'catch'. Van wondered if perhaps it had merely been placed there at a later date just to keep it safe.

"Okay, Jimbo, get out of here now."

Van waited for the door to close behind Jim, then brought the phone closer. It rang before he had a chance to pick up the receiver. It was Phil Johnson, a private detective from Corinth, the next town from Baseford.

"Hey, Van-man, I just ran across some info that might interest you. Could be connected to your robbery and missing person case."

Van hesitated. Phil was a good detective, but a little prone to taking credit for things he didn't do. *Was this a scheme to get info out of me*, he wondered?

"So ... are you interested or did you already solve the case by yourself, Superman?"

"No, hey, sorry Phil." I *Might as well run with this.* "You caught me in the middle of studying some mug shots. What've ya got?"

Van listened intently while the detective from the next town filled him in. While Phil wasn't positive there would actually be a connection, he'd heard a drunk blubbering the night before in a local bar. The guy's best friend was in trouble because of a robbery and he was the only one who knew where to find him.

"You know how they get to bragging sometimes. Well, my ears perked up at that, so I managed to get a couple of bar stools closer without him noticing. This guy was really stupid. Frankie, you know, the bar tender at the Old Mill Tavern, plunked a coke down in front of me and asked if I could use his help. Natch, I said sure. Frankie went back to the guy and started to challenge his story. By the time he got done, the dummy was mad and went into detail to prove it. He said he'd even brought a change of clothes to his friend the night before. Are ya still with me? Hate to be rattling on for nothing, here."

"Oh, yeah … of course." Van was not only hanging on to every one of Phil's words, but was furiously writing down notes on the back of an envelope. "Sounds like you've stumbled on to something. What else? More, I hope."

"Well, of course. Well, see, the guy was a heavy chain smoker. When he ran out of matches, he crumpled up the empty match book and tossed it on the floor. No big deal so far, you're saying, right Van?"

Van was hooked, good and proper. "C'mon, Phil. You know me better than that. I would have shut you up long before now if I didn't think it was relevant. You just keep rolling along. I might get lucky with this one."

"You mean 'we', I'm sure. Great. Like I said, the guy was looking around for something to light up the next cig. You know how considerate I am. Always helpful. Natch, I got up and offered him a light. Of course I dropped my lighter, reached down to pick it up and grabbed that matchbook at the same time. Pretty smooth, huh?"

Van sighed. If this was another one of Phil's practical jokes, he was dead meat in Van's eyes. But, somehow the tone of his voice sounded serious, so Van kept his cool.

"Okay, Phil. You did a great job. Yeah, I wish you worked for us here and all that crap you want to hear. Is there more? If so, get to the point, will you?"

Phil was quiet for a few seconds, probably drinking in the left handed compliment Van had delivered.

"Okay, wise guy. Back on track now. The guy didn't catch on to my trick and he was so happy to have a new listener, he kept on blabbing. It wasn't long before I started putting two and two together."

"And ... C'mon, Phil. I'm a busy man. What the hell did you find out?"

Phil sarcastically reminded Van that he could just as easily hang up the phone right then and do the investigating on his own. Van played along, slid in a short apology and begged him to continue.

"Well, here it is. I think you may know where the place is, Van-man. You remember the Lennox Crossing case where the rich dame was murdered?"

Van thought for a moment. "I wasn't here then, but I think it was six or seven years ago at that resort that's now closed, right?"

Phil answered, "Yep, that's the one. And that one's never been solved. Still open for us. That's all I've got. You fill in the blanks."

Van's heart was racing. He could fill in some blanks, all right. Of course. That's why the name was so familiar.

"The White Horse Inn. I read that she was found in the swimming pool, right?"

Phil cut in. "Bingo ...that's it. What do you think? Have we got something?"

"Christ, Phil, you may have found the clue of the century. I'm not kidding you, man. Can you meet me someplace tonight? I want to talk more about this, but someplace private."

Arrangements were made. Van started to get ready to leave, but remembered the phone call he had to make. He dialed the number. After five rings, he was just about to hang up when Anna answered. She sounded out of breath.

"Oh, Otto, I'm so glad you called. I was trying to wash my hair in the kitchen sink:. You know it's hard to hear anything else when you're doing that. Thank you for not giving up."

As usual, Van gleaned a gem of a lesson from his aunt. Always let the phone ring at least ten times. He reassured her while inwardly scolding himself for the impatience which had almost caused him to slam the phone down.

Van teased her. "So, Anna, have you been busy taxing your brain for me?"

Silence.

"Ummmm. Are you all right?" Another few seconds seemed to drag by, then Anna replied, "Just toweling my hair, dear. Did I miss something?"

"You'll be pleased to know I've been working most diligently on my homework. Whenever you have the time, I'll show you what I've done with my calendar."

Wow, Van was intrigued, but it was almost five o'clock. He had other things to do. As Anna would say, 'other fish to fry'.

"That's great. I'll call you tomorrow morning and we'll compare notes. I might have something new, too."

Van hung up and still had his hand resting on the telephone when it rang again. Tempted to ignore it and leave, he needed to know who was calling.

"Hello, Detective Van Hustler, here."

"Damn, I'm glad you're there." It was Gina.

Van was not so glad. Talking to her was ranked low on his list of things to do.

"What's up, Gina? I'm just leaving for a very important appointment."

Van fell silent for the next few minutes. He listened with amazement to what Gina told him. Her autopsy findings were not only a surprise, but something so bizarre that he found it hard to believe.

Gina gave him a quick report. "Yup. I don't like to give out info on the phone, so can you get your partner in crime and meet me at the morgue later on tonight? I'll stick around until 11."

He was torn. This was important news, but so might the information be that he was headed out to check on. Van hated to put her off. "Sorry, Gina. We'll have to do that tomorrow. Gotta chase a big lead right now."

Ten minutes later he switched off the office light and slipped quietly out his door. He walked as nonchalantly as possible past the water cooler, hoping no one would question him. He ducked out of the back door into the parking lot.

Chapter 7

It was already dark when Van pulled his MG into a parking space in front of Carl's Pub and Grub. He rummaged around in the pile of odds and ends lying on the passenger seat, looking for a notepad.

He nearly hit his head on the roof, when he was startled by a sharp rap on his window. Van automatically reached for his gun.

It was only Phil.

"Jesus, Phil, what are you trying to do, get yourself killed?"

Phil stepped back out of the way and Van peeled himself out of the little car.

"Hey, sorry, man. I thought you must have seen me standing right over there."

Van shook a fist at Phil and warned, "No shenanigans from you, understand? I'm not in the mood for jokes."

Phil raised both of his hands in surrender. "I'm good, Van. Don't shoot."

Van laughed, more at himself than at Phil. He didn't realize he was so uptight.

The two men shook hands and walked to the pub's front door. Van held the door open and made a gallant sweep with his free hand. "After you, kind sir."

Van didn't hear what Phil mumbled under his breath, but he assumed it wasn't that important. As soon as they entered, a buxom redhead rushed over to greet them.

"Well, hello, Phil. Haven't seen you in a dog's age." She grabbed Phil's face and gave him a big smooch on the lips, then lead them over to a booth near the back. "Nice and quiet back here, just like you ordered."

That sounded like Phil had called ahead. And the woman acted like she was very familiar with Phil.

After the woman took their drink orders, she gave Phil a long, questioning look, but Phil shooed her away.

Van couldn't help but ask, "Hey, what's with the gal? You didn't seem to back off when she planted one on you."

Phil told him it was a long story and an old one. "Her name's Janice. Skip it, okay?"

It was okay. Van was in a hurry to hear the whole of Phil's other, more important story, anyway.

"Let's get down to business, shall we? Let me see that matchbook."

Phil took a small plastic bag out of his coat pocket. "You mean this one?" He dangled it in front of him. "Oops, sorry ... no fooling around." He handed it over to Van.

Van recognized the words, 'white horse' right away on the matchbook, but there was something else in the bag. "And what's this junk," he asked as he shook the bag.

"Hey, stop playing with important evidence. That's the guy's cigarette butts. I grabbed the ashtray when Frankie brought it over and left it near me on the bar."

Van was impressed. "Nice work, Phil. We can use them to see if there's any traces on our murder victim ." And maybe other places, too, he thought.

Janice came back to the table with the drinks. Phil's was a double scotch and Van's was a light beer. Van scooped the plastic bag into his lap.

Janice laughed. "Yeah, better hide the evidence, right, Phil? Don't want some useless dame messing things up."

Van could almost feel the heavy hostility in her words. *Boy, Phil must have done that lady wrong,* he thought.

Phil turned red in the face and glared at her. Van was getting embarrassed, wondering if he was going to witness a brawl between the two of them.

Phil's manner changed. It was amazing to Van just how much.

"Now, Janice. You shouldn't talk like that in front of my friend." His voice was low, calm and steady. "I thought we had our problem all straightened out. Didn't we, Hon?"

Janice lowered her head and said, softly, "Yeah, Phil. I'm sorry mister." She turned toward Van and winked.

Somehow Phil had switched all the heat off and Janice was subdued. She turned around and walked away. The word 'sashay' was more like it. She had a lot of swing in her ample hips.

"How the hell did you do that, Phil? She looked livid."

"What does that mean? li-vid? You know you can't use those fancy college words with me. I'm just a street bum, remember?"

Phil insisted that they get off the Janice track and get back to the crimes. Van had to agree, but he was totally mystified about the former scene. What did Phil Johnson and sexy Janice have going in the past?

Van took the envelope with his notes from Phil's phone call on it out of his jacket pocket. They talked back and forth another twenty minutes about the possible connections between the new murder that Van was working on and what Phil knew about the unsolved one from the past.

It surprised Van that instead of Phil being a bother to deal with, they seemed to work quite well together. Phil's recall of the past murder was a big help.

They talked a few minutes more out in front of the pub and made plans to meet again soon. In fact, Van decided to take a chance and suggest to Anna that Phil should be included in their next discussion. *It's going out on a limb,* he thought. But he had a feeling it might work. Between Phil and Anna, who had both lived in the area longer than him, he hoped he could come up with more of the puzzle pieces faster.

As they parted, Van noticed Phil scan the front of the building and parking lot, then he jumped into his car and sped off.

Probably hoping Janice was not hanging around waiting for him, Van thought. Or, who knows, maybe it was just the opposite. Was he hoping to find her? Van had learned a long time ago that what a person said and did could be totally different.

He squeezed into his car and said, out loud, "If I had time to think about that, I'd find out what their mystery is."

"Who's mystery?" A woman's voice came from the left side of the building. He hadn't closed the car door yet, so it was very distinct.

Janice stepped out of the shadows and walked over to him. Van didn't know what to do. His first thought, 'flight'; slam the door shut and take off. Second thought, 'curiosity' kicked in.

"What's up, Janice? You missed Phil."

"Oh, I saw him leave. Good riddance."

The mystery expanded; the suspense tingled up his spine. Van was intrigued. At least enough to spend a little time right there in the open, safe and well lighted parking lot. Just as long as it would be a talk and no action.

"Okay, Janice. Did you want to tell me something?"

"Can't I come sit in your car? Much more comfortable."

Van repeated to himself, *talk, no action,* but the well bred gentleman in him won out. "Well, okay, but not for long."

Janice hurried around the car and pulled the door open. "Don't worry, I don't bite."

Van shrugged his shoulders, giving in to the inevitable. Janice was in the car. The point of no return had been marked.

"Again, please say what you want to say. I can't stay here long." Van did his best to set up the ground rules for the game.

"Oh, relax, junior. I'm not going to attack you. I get sore and shoot my mouth off sometimes, but I'm harmless. Just ask old Phil."

Van kept silent. He figured the less he said, the better.

"So, do you know anything about old Phil and me?"

Van just shook his head. No words. *Let her do all the talking and then get the hell out of here.*

"Well, yes, we had a good thing going, hot and heavy for a while about two years ago. To this day,

I don't know what happened or what changed his mind about me."

Van spoke. "So, you want me to find that out for you?"

Janice shook her head so hard, her large breasts, bound loosely in a light weight purple sweater bounced back and forth in the opposite direction of her head. "Hell no, it's way too late for that. I might want to know why, but I'm completely over him. Don't you worry about it. I've had plenty of attention from nicer guys since Phil."

Then what does she want, Van wondered? Wish she'd spit it out and get it over with. "Janice, what do you want from me?"

"Well," she crooned and moved closer to him.

Van was all of a sudden glad his car had separate bucket seats. He leaned back against the window.

Wrong move. Janice got up on one knee and leaned even closer. "I like you. We could have some fun together."

Van leaned toward the steering wheel just as Janice reached her left hand over to touch his face. "I … I don't think so," he said as he gently pushed her back by the shoulders. "I don't have a lot of time for fun."

She sat back down in her seat and sighed. Van adjusted himself straight forward in his. "Now, if that's all you wanted, then I think you should get out of my car now."

"Okay, I know when I'm not wanted, but you might change your mind about seeing me again."

Van was getting angry, but he sensed something else coming that could be important, so he let her continue.

"I just might know some things about stuff that happened in the past. Things others may not know."

Van perked up. "Like what?"

Janice shook her head again, but not so wildly this time. "Oh, no. It's not that easy. I don't give anything away for nothing, junior."

She opened her purse. Van stiffened, put his hand on the gun in his shoulder holster and held his breath.

Janice pulled a small piece of paper out and handed it to him. "Hey, relax, honey. I told you I'm harmless." With that she laughed and opened the car door. "That's my number. Give me a call if you change your mind."

Chapter 8

*I*t's nine o'clock in the morning. I've got a pile of work to do and I'm sitting on my aunt's couch. Van asked himself what was wrong with that picture, but he already knew the answer.

Just because a cup of tea was being made for him did not mean he was slacking off. Yes, he had crimes to solve and Anna could possibly be of help with the one that happened right there at Harrington.

The initial shock of the murder seemed to have worn off. Now Anna would be on guard, watching the girls, especially the new one, Kathleen. Any little clue that might be related would be jotted down in the three by five inch notebook that Anna always kept in the pocket of her smock. Van could count on that.

Anna claimed she wore smocks over her clothes for two reasons. One to keep her few, but expensive garments protected and two, to give her a more 'uniform' look in hopes of maintaining order in the school.

Van picked up the calendar that she had left on the coffee table for him. He was anxious to find some useful information. He found nothing.

"Oh, Otto, I can tell by the way you've got your face all scrunched up that you are disappointed." Anna put his cup and saucer on the coffee table.

"Well, a little bit. I thought you were going to use it to help retrace the last few weeks for me."

Anna pointed to the calendar. "If you look closely, you'll notice numbers on it. I didn't have room to write everything in those small spaces, so I just put numbers when I thought of something and wrote the details in my notebook. Pretty smart, huh?"

She grabbed a smock from the back of a dining room chair and fished around in the pockets.

Anna sat down on the couch next to Van, notebook in hand. "See, it's all neat and tidy in here."

Van tried to grab the little book, but she pulled it away. She shook her head. "No. Let me show you. Look at last month."

Van turned the calendar page back to October. "Okay, here's number one on October fifth. What does that mean?"

"That's the day, actually evening, that Kathleen arrived here. Let's see now," Anna said as she thumbed through the notebook pages.

Van sipped his tea and listened patiently while Anna told him about that night.

Kathleen Sullivan had been expected, but was supposed to arrive by noon. The cook and kitchen staff had prepared for at least one more and maybe three extra lunches. When three o'clock rolled around, Anna called the only contact number she had, but found it was not in service anymore.

"Nothing I could do but wait. I didn't worry, though. After all, they were coming from New York City. Anything could have happened."

Van chuckled. "Yeah, NYC's a scary place, isn't it?"

Anna just crossed her eyes at him.

Van was just teasing her. He knew she could probably count on one hand the number of times she had actually been there.

"Okay, I'm sorry. Go ahead."

Anna continued. "Around five thirty, a big black limousine pulled up to the school's front entrance. Two men got out. One was very young, probably in his early twenties and the other looked older and walked with a slight limp. I met them outside the front door."

"I asked them where Kathleen was and they assured me she was in the car but they wanted to bring her in through the back entrance with no outside lights on."

Van cut in. "Didn't you think that was weird? That would give me the creeps."

Anna agreed. She had been surprised about all the secrecy, but went along with it. She directed the men to the small parking lot in the back of the building and hurried down through the kitchen to turn off the spotlight.

The young man brought Kathleen in.

"I figured I would take her up to her room, but he asked how to get there. I was left standing in the doorway while he brought her upstairs, himself."

"Jeez, Anna, did he also give you orders about what he expected you to do? Sounds like they had some reason to hide her here."

Anna nodded. "Yes, that's true, but when he came back to the kitchen, he just said, 'Leave her alone. She'll be fine. Don't bother her.'

Then they left. The end. I tried to see if there was anyone else in the car, but the windows must have been those fancy tinted kind."

She stopped talking and shook her head.

Van gave her a couple of minutes, then asked if she was all right.

"Yes, I'm okay. It just amazes me that happened and I felt totally helpless. Completely unable to control the situation. That's not like me."

Van put his arm around her shoulder. "Were you afraid, maybe?"

"No … well maybe, but I was more shocked, I think. I wanted to go check on Kathleen; make sure she was all right, but the man told me to leave her alone, so I did."

Van asked her about the next day.

"That's number two in my notebook. Do you have time, Otto?"

He checked his watch. It was almost ten o'clock. He really didn't have any more time. Jim would be pacing around the station waiting for him.

"Wish I did, Anna, but I gotta go. You keep thinking and writing those notes. Good job, Detective Gorham."

He took a gulp of stone cold tea and stood up. Van promised to call her soon and walked over to the door.

"Maybe tonight. I think you're on to something big."

Anna blew him a kiss.

* * * * * * * * * *

As soon as Van walked into the police station, someone called his name. Jim had left a message to meet him at the airport.

"Why, what's up?"

It was Brad who answered the question. "Oh, you know Jimbo. Tight lipped as ever. He did mention something about the baggage claim office, though. Probably where he wants to meet you, I'd guess."

"Thanks, Brad. I'll be on my way. Tell him that if he calls, okay?"

Van remembered that his MG was running on fumes, so he signed out a squad car.

On his way to the airport, he found himself mulling over Anna's story of Kathleen's arrival. What the hell was that all about? And what happened the next day? If he had his way, he'd go right back and find out what the number two story was.

It only took Van ten minutes to get to the airport. He parked the car in the fire lane right out in front. Then he had second thoughts and moved it back about two car lengths to make room in case of emergency.

When he walked into the lobby, Van noticed Jim right away. He had a big coffee cup in his left hand and was waving wildly with his right. Van hurried toward him.

"Hey, what's up, Jimbo?"

"C'mon to the baggage office." Jim pointed to his right. " Got something' to show you."

Van followed . They turned a corner and came to the office door. Jim opened the door and called, "Hey, Charlie, I'm back. He went over to a half door.

"Detective Hustler's with me. Can we come back there?"

Van heard the sound of a buzzer and someone saying, "Sure, sure. C'mon in."

Jim opened the half door and Van stepped in behind him. The room they entered was filled with all kinds of luggage and plastic bags, beat up cardboard boxes and shelves along three walls filled with all kinds of items apparently left behind by passengers.

The man sitting behind the huge desk in the center of the room got up to greet them. He was a short, pot bellied guy with an almost bald head. The creases around his eyes deepened as he smiled and offered a pudgy hand to Van.

Jim introduced them. "Van, this is Charlie. If you want to know anything about what goes on in this building, he's your man."

Van was happy to hear that. "Always good to know someone on the inside, they say. Hi, Charlie."

Jim cut right to the chase. "Charlie, can you get that suitcase for us?"

Charlie reached under his desk and pulled out a small piece of luggage. It looked very old and overly used. The tan grass cloth covering was falling apart. A few of the loose cloth fibers swished in the air like a grass skirt when Charlie brought it up to the desk top.

"Hey, hey, hey. What do we have here," Van asked? "You know, Jimbo, if this was NYC, we'd have the bomb squad breathing down our necks."

"Yeah, I know, but I doubt if this is anything that dangerous. Well, it's not ticking anyway."

"Charlie," Van asked, "did you open it?"

Charlie shook his head. "No way, man. I don't have the authority to open anything around here. Except this office and the men's room."

Jim explained. The cashier in the coffee shop was ending her early morning shift and when she walked back to get her coat, she found this thing under the coat rack. She called Charlie and he retrieved it and brought it here.

"Then I called the station right away. Yessir, I don't waste time a-wonderin'. That's for you guys to do, right?"

Van assured Charlie that he'd done the right thing. "Thanks for acting so quickly, pal."

Jim picked up the case gingerly and brought it closer to him and Van. "Okay you or me?"

Van told him to go ahead. "But go easy....very slowly now."

Charlie took a few steps toward the door. "Hey, you guys mind if I just step into the waiting room?"

Van noticed Charlie was trembling. He probably shouldn't have mentioned the bomb squad. "Sure, but don't go any farther than that, please."

Jim undid one of the leather straps very carefully. Then he did the same with the second one. "Whew. I was afraid they'd fall apart on me."

He lifted the top slightly, then a little more and gradually flipped it back.

Van could see something that looked like a tiny baby's arm sticking out of a blanket. He took a sharp breath in and stepped closer. He was relieved to find it was only a baby doll.

"Man, that had me going for a minute, there."

"Yeah, me too. You thought it was a kid, too?"

Van took over. He picked up the blanket and doll so Jim could check the rest of the suitcase contents. There was a hand knit doll hat and a small plastic toy bottle.

"What's that thing?" Van asked, pointing to a round piece of fabric.

"Hah, it's a doll bib. Can tell you never had any kids." He picked up the bib and put it under his chin to show Van how it was used.

That's when Van noticed the folded piece of paper. It must have been under the bib.

"Look, wise guy ... that might be a note. Let me see it." Van handed the doll over to Jim and picked up the paper. He unfolded it and read the words to himself.

He winked at Jim and called Charlie back into the room. "It's okay, Charlie. We're taking this down to the station. Nothing to worry about."

Van slipped the note back into the suitcase. Jim packed up the doll and blanket, redid the straps on the case and they both rushed out of the half door as Charlie came in.

Van recognized the questioning look on Jim's face, but he shook his head and said, "Not here."

They didn't speak again until they were out of the airport.

Van handed Jim the note. "Here. You take all this down to the station and put it in my office. Check this note and see if the handwriting matches any of the letters we found in the locker."

"Okay, Boss, but where're you going?"

"I'm going to go hear story number two."

Van laughed as he caught the puzzled look on Jim's face in the rear view mirror.

Chapter 9

"Come in Otto." called the voice on the other side of Anna's apartment door.

How did she know it was me? God, she should be more careful, Van thought as he turned the doorknob and slowly pushed the door open. Once he had given the door a hefty shove to make sure no one was behind it, he stepped into her living room.

Still not totally sure she was safe, Van called from the open door, his hand on his unclipped shoulder holster. "Come out here so I know you're okay, Anna."

She popped around the corner from the kitchen with a cookie sheet in her towel wrapped hand. "My Lord, Otto ! What's gotten into you?" I'm fine. No boogey men here."

Van relaxed and came into the room. He exhaled with relief.

"We need to talk, Anna. Things around here may not be as safe for you as you think and I need to know everything that's gone on since that girl arrived. Not just in small chapters, but all of it, now."

Anna nodded. "Just let me take the rest of the cookies out of the oven and I'll come sit with you in there."

Van sighed and worked on setting up his full detective mode. He wanted his aunt to be more cautious, but he also didn't want to over frighten her.

"Okay, I'm ready'" she said as she bounced into the room. She placed a cookie into Vans open mouth. "Now I mean it, Otto. I know this is serious."

Van's thoughts ran for just a second to never being able to get used to her insistence to call him Otto, but quickly flashed back to the crucial subject.

He knew from years of experience that he could tell her almost everything that was happening on his end, but he had to convince her that she had to share every detail no matter how small, with him.

"Let's continue with your calendar notes. I'm hoping some of those will fill in some gaps in our investigation so far."

Anna reached for the calendar. "Let's see. Oh yes, we left off with the night Kathleen arrived. That was strange, wasn't it?"

"Yes … very strange … now what about the next day? Any notes for that?" Van scowled. He was anxious for clues and couldn't help showing it.

Anna thought a bit before she spoke. "Yes, but not too much. Kathleen did not come down for breakfast when the bell rang so I sent one of the girls up to rouse her. Ginny came back down to report that the "new girl" was awake, fully dressed, but not about to join us. Ginny was very indignant when she announced that Kathleen must have expected her meals brought to her. We all had a good laugh about that and enjoyed our breakfast."

Van asked, "Didn't you think that was unusual? But, no.....the girl arrived suddenly with no clue as to how things worked here, didn't she?"

"Of course. I made a mental note then to go visit her and give her an orientation tour. I did that right after breakfast."

Anna checked her notebook. "I found Kathleen just as Ginny had. Dressed and sitting on her bed. She declined the breakfast tray I brought. Claimed she never ate breakfast. No thank you, no smile.. It was like talking to a stone."

Van took over from there. He wanted to know more about the girl's demeanor, how she acted during Anna's attempts to help her acclimate to Harrington and mostly how Anna felt about her personality. His aunt was very good at quickly summing people up.

"Oh, that was interesting. And a shock to me at first. I expected some problems. Many girls don't arrive here willingly. But she came right out and told me she wouldn't be here for long, so she didn't want to know anything about the place. The only thing I accomplished was to get her to agree to at least come down for meals at noon and five. Cold as ice, she was."

Van questioned, "How did she act? Any body language signals? Did she use any bad language with you? "

Anna didn't have much to add except that she couldn't figure the girl out. "It was something I've never seen or felt before. Totally devoid of anything to give me a hint of how to treat her. No sass, no bad language, just short answers to my questions or no answers at all. And her face didn't change one bit when she did speak. Didn't move her arms, hands or legs, either. I've never seen so much control in a young person."

Van found Anna's description to be rather unreal at first, but then he was reminded of the face he saw the night of the murder. If that was the same girl, she was certainly smiling then. Not a friendly smile. No, more like a sneer. An icy sneer.

"All right, now what's the next thing," Van asked?

"Well, things were okay for a couple of days, then …"

Anna's phone rang. They both jumped. She answered it. "Yes, Jim, he's here. Hold on. "

"Okay, okay … calm down, Jimbo. What? No kidding. Of course, of course. I'll get there as fast as I can."

Van held on to the phone receiver for a few seconds, sorting out the news he had just heard.

Anna held her hand out to take it from him, an expectant look on her face.

No, Van decided, none of it was anything he could share with her just yet. He just shook his head. "Can't tell you … sorry."

He was up and over to the door by the time she had hung up the phone.

"Please Anna. Keep this door locked. I don't like the feel of what's happening here lately."

Anna nodded. "All right, Otto, I'll do that. I'm starting to feel it, too."

She went over to the door, hugged him and said, "I'll try to get some more information for you."

Van kissed the top of her head. "That would surely help, but be very careful, please."

He left, but waited just a few seconds outside her door until he heard the click of the lock and the slide of the chain.

I feel bad about not telling her, but even a watered down version of this is too involved to try to explain at this point.

Chapter 10

Thirty minutes later, Van met Jim at the station and they jumped into a squad car. On their way to the morgue, Jim drove while Van explained, "Gotta warn ya, Jimbo; this is no ordinary every day murder victim we're going to see. Sounds brutal, even to me. And I've seen a lot. Might be a shock to you."

Jim chuckled as he pulled into a parking space. "Don't worry about me, Boss. I can handle it."

Gina was waiting, but not patiently. "What the hell took you so long?" She put both rubber gloved hands out in front of her and added, "Never mind. No time."

As Van and Jim walked toward the examining table, she barked, "Gloves on."

She pointed to a counter to their right that had boxes of all sizes of exam gloves on top. "No closer 'til you do that."

Gina had worked all night on the examination and autopsy. If her discoveries had surprised her, she showed no signs of it. Even though Van considered her personality to be cold as ice, he knew that she was an expert in pathology and could have her choice of jobs. They were fortunate to have her.

The closer Van and Jim got to the table, the more Jim tucked himself farther and farther behind Van. After taking one look, he grabbed Van's arm and started to lose his balance.

"Steady, buddy", Van whispered as he kept Jim from collapsing. "I warned you."

The victim looked to be in his late forties to early fifties. His hair was an ordinary brown. His face looked like it had not been long since he shaved. Maybe four days at the most,

Gina brought their attention to what she described as the 'star of the show'. She pointed to something that looked like a piece of meat on the tray. "They lopped it off ."

Both men gasped. Van whispered, "Holy crap. This looks like a scene from that godfather movie."

Jim was barely peeking at what Van was describing.

Gina continued, filling them in on the details. As usual her voice was professionally calm and controlled. "As you can see, the penis looks raggedly cut. Like the killer was not an expert. Not only that, but it looks like the vic may have tried to chew on it to get it out of his mouth."

Jim started to buckle again. "Oh my God. That's awful. They really stuffed ... ohhhh.?"

Even Van was a little surprised at what he saw, but only because he didn't expect that kind of a vicious murder in a small quiet town like Baseford. His time in New York City had been full of tragic violence.

Jim seemed to go into a trance. His mouth hung open and he kept shaking his head.

Van poked him in the ribs and whispered, "Snap out of it, man."

Gina sighed in disgust. "Hey, when I talk, you dumb asses listen. Don't blame me if you miss something important."

Van apologized. "Sorry Gina. I think Jim's in shock. I'm listening."

"Fine. So that's the reason there was so much blood. He must have used his hands to try to get it out, too. That's why they are so bloody."

Van gulped and nodded. "Poor guy. Better off if he'd died right away."

Gina agreed . She tore her gloves off and threw them on the tray. On her way across the room, she shook Jim's shoulder. "Welcome to the real world, kid."

She stalked out the door and slammed it behind her.

Van and Jim quickly left the room, too. Jim's gait was a little shaky and he still held onto Van's arm until they reached the car..

"Jimbo, are you going to live, man?"

Jim took his hand off Van's arm and brought it down to his crotch. "My God. I can't stop thinking of that thing sitting on the tray. And that's one scary lady, too."

Van laughed and replied, "Calm down, buddy. She may be a royal pain in the ass, but she's a top notch professional. Chalk it up to a major piece of your learning curve,"

Jim couldn't let it go. "I just can't imagine someone doing that.. Damn !!"

Van COULD imagine it all. The man held or tied down, seeing the knife. He could almost feel the mounting terror, the pain, the gagging, the choking.

"Yeah, I've seen it before in New York. I don't want to freak you out, but most of the time it IS done while the guy is still alive. It's my guess that happened to this poor bastard, too. I only hope he lost consciousness quickly."

Jim just kept saying, "Oh my God. Oh my God."

Van was on a roll. "And sometimes they don't kill the victim and he lives. That's sad. And let me tell you about what somebody did to a young nun …"

"Stop, Van. Please. I'm Catholic, you know !!"

The ride back to the station was silent. Van tried to push the recent findings back into his mind's memory bank and clear his thinking. His growing concern for Aunt Anna moved into the forefront.

The next problem would be what and how much to tell her. *Gory is gory; no way to make it pretty,* he thought.

Once they got to the station, Van told Jim he wanted to get back to see his aunt. "I'm getting worried about her safety now. Check with the chief and see if you can come with me."

While Van waited in the car, he tried to figure what he could and would tell Anna about this end of the bizarre situation. *Nope. No details about the murder yet.* When Jim came out of the station he looked pasty white. Van decided to drive.

"You look awful, Jimbo. Are you sure you want to do this?"

Jim shrugged his shoulders. "Yeah. The chief said I looked so bad, I could go home and get some rest, but I'll be okay."

On the drive over to the boarding school, Van's peripheral vision caught the motion of Jim's frequent head shakes.

He parked the car right at the school front entrance. "Okay, time to check in with Anna and see if she has anything new to tell us."

Jim cringed. "Okay, but would you mind telling me why you parked here? Pretty obvious, isn't it?"

"Yup. First I want to let Anna know we're here. And if the girls notice we're here, maybe that Kathleen will react somehow."

He opened the car door. "C'mon with me. Anna will be glad to see you and you can help prevent me from giving her too much info before it's necessary."

"Oh yeah. I know how that can happen easily with her. And this time, I don't want to hear it, either."

As they entered the front door and walked over to the ornate grand double staircase, Van wondered if his aunt was even in her apartment at that time or still in her office. He decided to try the apartment.

Chapter 11

It was more likely that she was in the school section at three o'clock in the afternoon, but he had other things to check in the dorm, anyway.

Anna's apartment was at the far end of the second floor dorm rooms. To get there, they had to pass by five other rooms on each side of the corridor. Van pointed to the first door name plate and whispered, "Look for one marked "Kathleen".

When they got to the end of the hall, Van turned to face Jim. "I just saw one without a name. Might be hers, " he commented.

Still facing Jim, he reached one hand backwards to knock on Anna's door.

He nearly fell into her arms. She had already opened it..

Once Van regained his balance, he questioned her about locking the door.

"Of course," Anna answered. I saw you drive up and I've been waiting right here like a good little girl, listening 'til you got to my door. By the way, I could have saved you some time. Kathleen's room is on the next floor."

"How did you know it was us?"

"Oh, Otto, I'd know your raspy whisper anywhere. I figured you would be checking names on the doors, right?"

Van grimaced and Jim chuckled. Both knew that she was the only one who could get away with using his given name.

"Her room is right above my kitchen. So far, whenever I've been here, she's been quiet as a mouse. It sounds like she has been on the phone a few times, though. She must have a cell phone."

Van heard a timer bell ring in the kitchen. Anna left them standing in the doorway.

"Oh, my chicken is done. I'll be right back. Have a seat.."

Van motioned to Jim to sit and started to sit on Anna's couch. "Wow, good thing I looked first. She's turned this thing around since I was here this morning."

Jim gestured with both hands. "Why ?"

"Well, I guess she believed me when I told her she might be in danger and to lock her door.."

Anna came back to the room and stood next to Van. "I see you noticed the couch. I do feel better with it facing the door for some reason."

Jim questioned, "Did you move that all by yourself?"

"Silly question, Jimbo." Van chuckled. He knew his aunt was soon going to be sixty one, but she had always taken good care of herself and was strong and healthy. But for her to be concerned enough to move the couch meant that something had changed at the school..

Van reached over and touched Anna's hand. "Did something happen today?"

Anna squeezed his hand and crossed the room to sit in her rocking chair. She settled a bit then explained. "Not so much happened. It's more like my feeling that the atmosphere has changed around here. The girls seem nervous and jittery."

Jim cut in. "Couldn't that be simply because of the murder?"

"Yes, at first I did just chalk it up to that, but I think there has been some interaction between some of the girls and Kathleen."

Van started to speak, but Anna continued, "I'll check it out tomorrow, first thing. Don't worry."

"Okay, Anna, but", Van cautioned, "please be extra careful."

He was merely reciting the usual cautionary police words. He reminded himself, once again that Anna had assisted in cases before and pretty much knew the ropes, when to back off and when to jump in.

Jim stood up and gave Van a half salute. "I think we have to get back to the station soon, right, Van?"

"Oh yeah. Okay Anna. Thanks, and by the way, there will be some extra officers around here for a few days."

Anna perked up. Her enthusiasm and curiosity awakened. She asked, "Really? Are they looking for something in particular?"

Oh, boy, thought Van. Here we go.

Jim forcefully cleared his throat to stop Van from being too explicit in his answer, then decided to supply the information, himself. "Just a few personal things that are missing. You know, like a wallet, watch. You know, things like that to help us identify the victim."

Whew, that was close, thought Van. He stood up, went over to Anna and bent down to give her a hug so she wouldn't try to get up. He winked at Jim.

Once they were back in the squad car, Van thanked his partner. "I still feel like a little boy when she questions me. Jeez. She taught me to tell the truth or else."

"Well, Van, the details of this murder search would be difficult to explain to anyone, I think, especially to that dear lady."

* * * * * * * * * *

Jim drove to the station while Van tried to create in his mind how he would go about organizing the search. He figured that once he was able to get past the actual explanation to Chief Rocket of what the object was. The rest would be easy. Suddenly it dawned on him. "Holy crap, Jimbo. It's been two days and I haven't shared any of this case with the chief. He'll be so pissed !"

"Yeah, boss. I wondered when that was going to happen. We should do that soon, right?"

Van thought, *This case has been so close to a gangland slaying that I must have slipped into my old New York City tactics, keeping the clues to myself until I figured there was enough to make it stick.*

"I'll bet Gina has already filled him in from her end", Jim said. We are going to be in deep shit."

Van guessed that the chief would send him to New York pretty soon, so Jim would have to be part of the search.

"I know what you're thinking, Van. You'll be off to NYC and I'll be stuck with the bloody search." He cringed. "Yikes, that wasn't funny."

As it turned out, Van didn't have to explain anything after all. When they walked through the station entrance, they found the entire Baseford police force of seventeen men and three women gathered.

Stan Rocket was shouting orders. "Jim here; nice of you to show up, will lead the search. Meet here at o-six hundred tomorrow."

"Our shining star, Van is going to take a little trip to New York City. I'll see you in my office, Van !"

The chief continued in his staccato style.

"Okay, um …

Oops, almost said 'men' …

Folks …
People …
gals and guys …
Whatever …
Get some rest …
Long day tomorrow …
Dismissed."

Jim and Van made a bee-line for the chiefs' office door.

He charged across the room right behind them. He pushed them both roughly into the room. "What the hell, guys. How long were you going to keep this stuff secret?"

Laid out on a white table were all the things Van had stashed in his own office. "Honest, Chief, I was planning to give it all to you tonight."

Chief Rocket was angry and Van knew he had every right to be. "I don't know how they did things in the city, but here, we all share everything, all the time. Got that fancy guy?"

Van nodded. Jim stood behind him. His head lowered to his chest.

"And you, big shot. Did you forget everything you were taught before this guy showed up?"

"No, sir, " they both mumbled in unison.

Rocket went on. "Time to split you guys up. Van, go home and pack. You're going to trace the leads by finding that letter writer or writers. Get the first train out of here you can."

"And, Jim, you're leading the search tomorrow, for however long it takes."

He put both hands, open palmed out in front of him. "Now I'll take anything and everything else you have been hiding that has to do with this case."

Van was caught. Should he give Stan the match cover from the inn that he still had in his pocket? He weighed it back and forth in his mind, then decided to go with his gut.

Maybe the three cases really weren't related? What if that lead threw them off course, wasted precious time? Better to hold it until after the New York trip. Decided. Done deal.

Van looked over all the items on the table. "Looks like you got everything out of my office, Chief." He motioned to Jim. "See anything missing?"

Jim caught the intent in Vans' voice. "Nope, Jeez, I didn't know we had so much already."

The chief made them explain every piece of evidence on the table. "And you better tell me everything you know about the case. This is a serious murder."

It was after eight-thirty p.m. when Chief Rocket ordered them out of the room, then remembered something. "Oh yeah, Van. Just so you know; I'll be personally leading the investigation at the school and that includes grilling your aunt. Do not, and I mean this, do NOT contact her before you leave."

Van had done his best to spare her the gory details, but it was out of his hands, now. He hoped she would cooperate and share all her findings with Stan.

Chapter 12

It seemed like no time at all and Van found himself on a commuter train to New York City. The chief sent him, of course, because his former job was with the NYC Police Department.

Van settled into his seat. Within five minutes he was eyeballing every passenger. The flashy blonde in the red coat, the little guy with the huge duffle bag, that bratty kid with the homely looking uniformed nanny.

Van's thought clicked back to the blonde. *Where was she going?*, he wondered. *Why was she so dressed up this early in the morning?* It didn't take long for him to come up with all the old familiar reasons.

Soon he was wondering where each passenger within his sight was going. Were any of them suspects? Did anyone on that car have anything to do with his case? Finally it dawned on him.

Snap out of it, Stupid. This is only one train car. One small group of people in a giant fish bowl. What are the odds one of them could possibly be involved in a small town murder?

Van took his own advice and tried to relax. Past memories drifted into his mind of friends who had been part of his life in the city. Cal and Judy popped up right away. Judy was a floating dispatcher for several precincts and Cal was a plainclothes detective. He and Sheila had tried to arrange double dates with them, but weren't often successful

All of us too busy, conflicting schedules. What a crazy life that was.

Van couldn't help falling back into thoughts of Sheila. Maybe she had the right idea. He remembered questioning his own career choice once when she had given up a high powered executive position and become a missionary. *I knew I wasn't made of missionary stuff.*

Whenever Van let those thoughts in, he always ended up in the same place. A vision of Sheila walking off into nowhere. It frightened him a lot.

Determined to try to enjoy the ride, Van pulled a paperback book out of his jacket pocket. "Cooking for One" had been a gift from Anna when he had first moved to Baseford. He agreed with her that a healthier diet would be better for him, but he wasn't quite ready to stand at a stove and actually prepare a meal back then. He doubted he was ready yet, but it was the only small book he had.

It was no use. The words on the pages were just helter-skelter. He couldn't make sense of them.

Then images replaced the words. The girl under the horse chestnut tree, the women at the airport locker, the distorted face of the dead man, the horrific sight at the morgue and the letters in his suitcase with the NYC return address.

Van couldn't shut off the movie playing in his head. The same clips, each taking only seconds continued to play over and over.

The born detective in him was obviously not going to allow any slacking off. Van recognized this phenomena as the familiar stage one of his normal way to connect pertinent facts. He'd often wondered if any other detectives had this happened.

Might as well go with this, he decided and closed his eyes. Was there already a connection he had missed? The girl, the women, the vic, the letters. Then again; the girl, the women, the vic, the letters. Round and round the same pictures waltzed. It reminded Van of a circus ring. The girl, the women, the vic, the letters, and …

On one of the rotations, Anna appeared. Her voice was soft, but clear. "Remember what I told you about solving mysteries, Otto? All the clues are like links of a chain. Each one, each detail as important as the other. Your nemesis is the catch. The one thing that will complete the circle and hold the chain together. What you are looking for is the catch."

He was a little boy. They were playing a mystery board game. "Now let's go over it again." Anna's voice trailed off.

The girl, the women, the vic, the letters. The parade was back.

Van was free of the images only when the commuter train made its stops along the way. Even though he knew it was only a habit, he couldn't help glancing at every passenger who walked by him.

At one of the stops he forced himself to turn his head and look out the window. A huge collection of trash was piled near the tracks. Van felt anger and disgust at the individual who had thoughtlessly dumped a tattered love seat over a tall fence. He supposed the jerk had no idea that it was now precariously balanced upside down on the scrawny limbs of a tree that would have no chance of surviving under the weight. *Out of sight, out of mind, I guess,* he thought.

At the next stop he saw some old car tires scattered like gravestones in their own little cemetery. Most were the ordinary type, but here and there he spotted the white necks of old abused whitewalls.

Graffiti was everywhere. Sheila's voice floated back to him. "Most of it is protest of something; living conditions, poverty, opposing street gangs full of anger." Almost all of it was in Spanish, the language she told him he should learn if was going to stay in the city.

Another thing she was right about, he realized. But he chose to get out, instead.

Once in a while Van noticed a mural done with skill and care. A celebration of an ethnic background. He had to agree with her. *Maybe there is still hope and pride to be found amidst the seemingly gruesome bowels of the cities.*

The scene Van saw before he got off the train was some repair work in progress under the canopy of the station roof. Sparks from a welding torch on a lower level cast an eerie light on the worker. He looked like a ghost over a witches caldron in a dark cave. He registered that picture as another sign of possible redemption for all the cities.

Van tried desperately to get memories of Sheila out of his mind, but he couldn't do it. When the train crept slowly into Grand Central Station, he had even begun to wonder if she still cared for him.

He sighed, stood up and stretched his long legs. As he reached overhead to get his suitcase, he shook his head as if to clear cobwebs.

Whew, this train ride has gotten to me. Time to stop thinking about Sheila and get to work !!

Chapter 13

Once Van was out on the street, he quickly made his way to the nearest local police station. The sights and sounds of the city blasted his senses.

Horns blared, drivers cursed and made gestures from open car windows, pedestrians yelled at drivers who came within inches of them as they tried to cross the streets. Everywhere, clouds of warm breath meeting cold air flew about. *No friendly home town smiles here,* he thought.

Van was surprised with his initial reaction. He felt suffocated by a dense fog of anger and bitterness. He pulled his jacket collar up around his neck. Funny, he didn't recall having that feeling when he lived and worked there.

He shielded his eyes from the sun with one hand and looked up to check a street sign. He saw a woman leaning out of a third story window. She was waving her arms and shouting.

He strained to listen "Help him," she screamed.

Van yelled back, "Who? Help who?"

"In the alley," She pointed to Van's right. Her eyes met his and riveted directly to his conscience. "Over there. Hurry !"

There was no way out of it. That woman was expecting his help and through mere eye contact he had promised to try.

Van took a couple of steps back to the alley he had just passed, automatically patting his chest on the left side to check his shoulder holster.

Christ, I don't even have my gun. It was still in his suitcase. He wasn't prepared to help anyone.

He stopped short at the corner of the building and just listened. At first the cacophony of city noise was all he could hear, but he quickly picked up the distinct sounds of trouble.

He peered cautiously around into the alley. There were three of them. Three guys beating up on one young boy.

Van's blood began to boil, but could he, or better yet should he try to go it alone?

"Hell, no time to get help," he growled as he dropped his suitcase and stepped into the alley. Wondering if it might be the last time he would say it, he dropped his suitcase and yelled, "Police. Break it up !"

Within seconds, the three men scattered into the shadows. Van welcomed his own sigh of relief when he found it unnecessary to tangle with the attackers.

He mentally patted himself on the back. The first twinge of self satisfaction was for scaring the thugs off. The second was for not pursuing them unarmed into the dark maze of unfamiliar alleys and buildings.

"Man, you timed that right." a gruff voice shouted from behind Van. A thin young man brushed past him, heading for the groaning boy.

Van turned around to see who had spoken and found a small group of young people.

He could feel the heat of embarrassment flare from his neck to his face as the realization hit him. Instead of his own formidable presence on the scene, their timely arrival had most likely been what really sent the bad guys packing.

A murmur of soft thanks surrounded Van as he walked out of the alley as quickly as possible.

* * * * * * * * * *

The nearest police station was only three blocks down the street, but when Van got to the next corner he turned left.

"Damn," he swore as he reached the waterfront and stopped at an old bench.

"Damn," again when Sheila's voice taunted him. *Darling, Van.* She always called him that. It always took him off guard; always pulled him away from his work world like a magnet.

"Damn." This time it was out loud and with a soft cry. Her last words to him from that bench came stabbing back into his heart.

"Van, Darling, you know there is no other way. You must stay to do your work and I must leave to do mine."

She was right, of course. He couldn't give up his job, his life in the city and she couldn't throw away the opportunity to do God's work as a missionary in Scotland.

"Case closed," he shouted to nobody. "Leave me alone!"

Van turned around and smacked himself on the side of his head. *Why do I do that to myself?*

He ran through a familiar alley to get back to the street leading to the station.

* * * * * * * * * *

The first thing Van did in the squad room, while telling the chief about the scuffle with the young people was to get his gun and holster out of his suitcase and strap it on.

Chief Flannery said nothing until Van was finished and looked settled. "Well, hello to you, too, Detective VanHulster. Welcome to the club."

Before he got a chance to continue, Van cut in. "Van, please. Call me Van."

The chief called two of his squad detectives into the office. "This is a detective from Baseford. A little town whose claim to fame is only an old boarding school for rich girls. And, by the way, he wants to be called Van for some reason, okay?"

Van couldn't miss the condescension in the chief's voice. *He has no clue who I am or that I had worked in the next precinct. Good. That might be an advantage. No expectations.*

He looked closely at the two detectives. Neither one registered any recognition. Again, Van was happy with that. Better to keep things clear and get on with the work.

The young man with the sandy crew cut said, "No prob, Van. What can we do for you?"

Van dug the plastic bag of letters out of his suitcase and explained that his next step was to find the address printed on the letters. He tucked the suitcase behind the row of desks.

"I'm Cliff. I'll go with you . Okay, Chief?"

"Yeah, yeah", he said and waved them out of the office.

Van asked, "Whew, is he always that friendly? Doesn't seem too happy to have me around."

"He's okay once he gets to know you, but kinda protective of his own. Calls us his kids."

Van understood this completely. It had been the same in his station back then. "That feeling hasn't changed much since I worked here in the city, then."

Cliff seemed genuinely surprised. "No kidding. Where did you work?"

Van explained that he had lived in one of the nearby buildings and worked as a detective in the next precinct. He told Cliff he was surprised that no one recognized him at the station. "And I didn't see anyone I knew, either."

Cliff was quiet for a minute, then told Van there had been a shake up there. "Big scandal, drugs, firings, the whole bit. We ended up with a new chief and almost a new squad. Charlie Davis and I are the only original guys."

Van asked him if Charlie was the other detective he'd been vaguely introduced to.

"Yeah, we're the only ones who know the area well, but Charlie's sorta shy. He's a great partner, but not one for volunteering right away."

Van understood. He'd had a couple guys like that in his squad, too.

He opened the bag and showed one letter to Cliff. "The return address looks like it's a few blocks off the Manhattan garment district. Either Snell or Skell."

Cliff nodded. "Yup. Know the area well. Used to work for a tailor down there while I was in high school. But that name doesn't sound familiar."

The news that Cliff was interested and knew his way around gave Van a lift. He was lucky to not be stuck with a stodgy detective who really didn't want to bother with someone's small town stuff.

When they came to the center of the district, Cliff called Dispatch and asked for a Snell Street location.

No luck, but there was a Sherell street five blocks west of them.

"Oh yeah, that's the street I walked down to get to work . Lots of small businesses there back then." Cliff seemed to be perking up, getting a little excited about the case.

Sherell Street turned out to be as Cliff remembered. Mostly small storefronts with some numbered doors that looked like residences. The return address had no number, so Van and Cliff started at the beginning of the street. One on each side with a letter for reference.

Van was about three quarters of the way down when he found a closed tailor shop that had a faded name on the door. The name matched the initials used on the letters.

"Cliff, come over and check this for me."

Cliff agreed. "Sure looks like it. Come to think of it, I remember a woman tailor lived here. My boss always complained that she would take all his customers away. No chance of that. He had all the right connections."

Van knew what that meant. Any business sponsored by the neighborhood bosses was guaranteed to prosper while others would eventually fail.

"Okay, Cliff. We're on to something. Next stop, City Hall. Let's dig up the past history of this mystery woman."

Chapter 14

At the city hall, Van headed over to the information desk. Out of the corner of his eye he saw that Cliff was already on the stairs. The clerk directed Van to the Registrar of Deeds office on the second floor.

Van joined Cliff. "Looks like you already know where we're going, Cliff."

Cliff chuckled. "Yep. I've done this a few times."

Of course he has, how stupid of me to assume I had to take charge.

"Sorry. Force of habit, I guess."

Cliff shrugged it off and took the stairs two at a time. "C'mon. This way."

A woman's voice greeted them from one of the desks as soon as they entered the brightly lit office. "I'll be right with you."

And she was. The pretty dark haired woman said, "Hi Cliff. How are you doing?"

Clearly they know each other. This could be helpful, Van thought.

Cliff introduced them. "This is Barbara Cronin. Not only the prettiest, but the sharpest one in the office. Meet Van. And I can't pronounce his last name."

Van found himself blushing when he noticed that Barbara was, too. He also couldn't help noticing that she was, indeed very pretty. He didn't know why he always expected office clerks to be frumpy.

She flashed a beautiful smile. "Pay no attention to him. He flatters all the women. I'm no expert, but I can probably help you find what you need."

Van explained what he was hoping to find. Barbara politely excused herself and went to the records vault. The huge ledger she returned with looked heavy and almost as big as she was.

She heaved it up with a slight grunt and plunked it on the counter separating them.

"Let's try five years back. She found the date tab for that and turned the ledger around so Van and Cliff could both read as she turned the pages.

It was a slow process and Van read the lines as quickly as he could, hoping Cliff would see something familiar.

They decided to go back another five years.

While Barbara was finding the ten year tab, Van had a chance to look at her more closely. Her short curly reddish hair complemented her fair complexion. Her head was down, but Van couldn't help noticing the freckles sprinkled over her cheekbones.

She turned pages and he and Cliff scanned for another half hour, but he saw nothing to give him any clues. When they got to the last page. he noticed it was dark out and looked up at the wall clock, then he heard the sounds of people closing up and leaving the building.

"Oh, gosh. Isn't it closing time? I'm sorry to keep you."

"Yeah, Barb", Cliff added. "We can come back tomorrow morning, right, Van?"

She shook her head. "No, that's all right. I'm intrigued. If you can give me a ride home, I'd like to keep going with this."

Van was very happy to hear that. Finding something that night was high on his priority list. "How about you, Cliff? Can you stick around?"

Cliff couldn't stay. He was already late to clock out at the station and had plans for the evening. "Cabs around here are a dime a dozen, though, so you should be okay."

Questioning glances darted between them all for a few seconds and Cliff left. As he went out the door, he said, "I trust you'll take good care of the lady, Van."

He and Barbara repeated their scan until they reached the fifty year page and decided that it wasn't worth going back any further.

Barbara suggested that he might be able to get more information by talking to the people in the neighborhood. "At least that's what I see them doing on TV."

Of course she's right. But I had hoped to do it the easy way and get right back home.

It was then that he noticed he was hungry and wondered if Barbara was, too. "I'm famished and you must be hungry, too by now. Is there someplace nearby where I could buy you some supper?"

Whoa, what the heck am I doing? I hope she isn't mad.

To his surprise, she accepted. And humorously, at that. "Ordinarily I would never do this. But I trust Cliff. He wouldn't have left me alone here with you if he hadn't already sized you up and put you in his 'OK' category."

That left Van in her control next because he had no clue where to go. Barbara knew of a diner just two blocks from there that was open day and night.

* * * * * * * * * *

Kelly's Diner was one of those places that looked like every other Van had ever been in. It even had that distinctively underlying smell of a recent disinfectant floor washing.

As he and Barbara walked in, a young man was cleaning a table to their right. "Hi, Miss Barbara," he said. "Long time no see."

She waved. "Hey Joey. Good to see you're still here."

The young man cowered and looked toward the kitchen.

Looks like the kid hoped his boss didn't hear that, Van thought, sensing a note of fear in his face.

A stout waitress was behind the counter making fresh coffee. She turned and shouted. "Wow, look who's here, Wes!"

The gruff voice coming from the kitchen was not the friendliest. "Yeah, where the hell have you been, young lady?"

Barbara didn't answer, but just gave a quick look toward the kitchen and walked into a welcoming hug from the waitress.

"Forgive him, honey. His memory ain't so great nowadays. How're you makin' out?"

Barbara answered, "Oh, I'm okay, Sue. I'm fine."

Sue steered them to a table in the back left corner of the room.

Good, Van thought. *Not too close to the kitchen or the toilets.* But true to his detective liking he would have been happier near a back entrance. *You never know when you might have to get out fast.*

Van was curious about Barbara and Sue's short conversation. He really didn't know anything about the new woman in his life. They had both been so totally wrapped up in the search, neither one had asked anything about the other's personal life. It sounded like she had some problems that Sue knew about.

Should he ask? How would he ask?

Sue interrupted his quandary. "Coffee? Two?"

Van nodded, yes, Barbara said, "No thanks. Tea for me, Sue."

When Sue went to get the drinks, Barbara leaned toward Van and whispered, "Is it okay to talk in front of her about your case?"

Van reassured her. Not only did he plan to talk about it. But he intended to ask Sue some questions. "Does she live anywhere near that street?"

When Sue came over with their drinks, Barbara surprised Van by questioning Sue herself. "Do you still live in that cute apartment on Carver Avenue?"

"Yes, yes I do. I just had the living room painted."

Barbara continued, "Isn't Carver a block from Sherell?"

A loud throat clearing echoed from the kitchen. Sue yelled, "Don't freak out, Wes. There are no other customers out here."

She took their orders. Van was so hungry he wanted everything on the menu, but he narrowed it down to meatloaf, gravy, mashed potatoes and peas. Barbara had eaten some lunch, so opted for a grilled cheese sandwich.

Sue asked, "Tomato on it, like usual?"

Barbara declined. "Not this time, thanks."

By then it was clear to Van that the two women knew each other fairly well. He decided to make the most of that and asked Sue if she knew anything about the building on Sherell Street.

She did, indeed remember the place. Her own grandmother had worked in the main building when it was a clothing factory. The small shop in front had been rented by a woman tailor who worked for the factory but also had her own customers.

When Sue called their orders through to the kitchen, the cook called her in. He wanted to talk to her.

It was so quiet in the dining room that both Van and Barbara could easily hear some of what the cook was saying to Sue. His voice was extremely loud. He demanded to know what Van had asked about.

Sue's voice was soft but her answer must have been sassy because the sound of a heavy pan being smacked down hard on a counter rang through the room. "You keep your damn mouth shut, girl !!"

Van jumped up, ready to go to Sue's defense. Barbara put her hand on his arm. "Don't worry, Van. Sue can handle Wes."

It got very quiet in the kitchen. Van strained to hear what was going on, but all seemed settled down to normal food preparation noises.

Soon Sue came out of the kitchen with their meals on a large tray. She was smiling, but Van could see she was visibly rattled. Her hands trembled slightly when she transferred the plates to the table.

Barbara and Van exchanged glances and both shook their heads.

No more questions. Don't want to start any more trouble for this lady.

Barbara understood the exchange and jotted her phone number on the corner of a paper napkin and stuffed it into Sue's apron pocket.

Chapter 15

As soon as Van closed the restaurant door and he and Barbara were out on the sidewalk, he asked her if Sue would be all right left there with Wes. "He sounds like a mean one."

"Oh sure. They've been together for many years. To use an old cliché', 'his bark is worse than his bite'. She can handle him."

"Okay, if you say so. Another cliché, is he a 'rough, tough cream puff?'" Van was surprised at how easy it was to kid around with Barbara.

They both laughed out loud. Barbara's laugh sounded to Van like a thousand tinkling bells.

She tried to stop. "Should we be having this much fun when working on a murder case?" The bells sounded once again.

Van did his best to be serious, too, but to no avail. "I'll chalk it up to nerves. That happens. But your laugh makes me laugh more."

Barbara looked into the restaurant window to see if Sue might have seen them acting so silly. "Okay, that's enough, now." She seemed to literally swallow the next giggle.

Van hailed a cab. Barbara told the driver her address.

Van wished he could write that down, but he didn't want to seem too obvious. *Or interested,* he thought.

Once they got to the building she lived in, Van walked her into the main lobby. They decided on a meeting time for the next day at City Hall. It was Saturday and she wasn't working, but wanted to help anyway.

Barbara surprised him with a quick kiss on his cheek, then hurried over to the bank of elevators. She waved as a door opened for her.

That was strange. And here I was worried about being too forward.

Van jumped into the cab and directed the driver to the police station. He hoped he would remember her address. *Why does it matter,* he wondered as he touched the spot on his cheek where she had kissed him.

He had to admit it. He was attracted to her. But it was just a few hours ago that he was stressing about missing Sheila.

"Women", he grumbled.

"What's that buddy?", the driver asked. "You got women trouble?"

Van chuckled, "Nah. I'm the trouble."

As soon as Van had paid for the ride and was walking into the station, he realized he had been so busy that he hadn't made any plans for a place to stay. *I feel so much at home here. Just assumed I'd be going to my old apartment, I guess.*

It was a whole new group of officers that greeted Van when he looked around. The squad shift had changed so he started to introduce himself and explain why he was there.

Chief Flannery's office door opened and he came out. "Well, if it isn't Van the man. Are you lost?" He chuckled and light laughter circled the room.

Van was tired and was getting sick of the attitude. He decided to clear the air.

He waved both hands in the air and yelled. "Okay, enough is enough. Look, my name is Sergeant VanHulster from the Baseford New York police department. I don't know why you weren't notified, but I'm working on a very important murder case and I would appreciate some cooperation. Does anyone have a problem with that?"

The room got quiet. Van continued. I've made plans to pursue some leads first thing in the morning, but right now I need some rest, so a suggestion for a place to stay in this area would help."

The chief spoke up. "C'mon in my office, Sergeant."

Once inside, Flannery quickly apologized. "We're all a little edgy here. I'm new at this and still working out how to keep the guys in line. So far they seem to like my blustery act, but I can see it doesn't work for you."

Nope, no help at all, Van thought as he took a deep breath to calm himself down.

The chief was working the night shift, so he offered to bring Van to his own apartment just three blocks away. He reached behind his desk for Vans suitcase.

He handed it to him. "I'll drive you over there, myself whenever you're ready."

Van nodded his head to the repeated, 'sorry'. "Okay, I'm more than ready, Chief."

After a short explanation to the squad, Flannery directed Van out the back door to the parking lot.

The chief put the flashing lights on, but not the siren. "Just to get you there faster."

Van's eyes were already almost closing, but he wanted to fill the chief in on the case. Flannery was familiar with the area and vowed to do some research that night for him.

Chief Flannery's apartment was much larger than Van had expected. He was too tired to look around and only interested in a bed and a bathroom. He knew he had walked through at least two rooms to get to those.

Once Van was settled in the bedroom, the chief handed him the key. "My desk number is on the nightstand if you need anything. I'll be home right after seven a.m.. Do you want me to wake you up before then?"

A groggy head shake was all Van could muster as he fell backwards on to the bed.

* * * * * * * * * *

Van woke up to the smell of coffee. He sat up and immediately noticed he was fully dressed. That puzzled him but the coffee aroma seemed more important. It wasn't until he put his feet on the floor that he realized the room was totally foreign.

A voice from another room called, "Van. Time to get up, I think. Follow my voice if you want coffee."

Van rubbed his eyes and did just that. The voice was singing 'Three Blind Mice'.

Van chuckled as he recognized Chief Flannery's voice, then the song. The memory of the night before drifted back into his mind.

The kitchen wasn't far away, but he went the wrong way down the hall and had to backtrack.

"Cream? Sugar?", Flannery asked as he handed Van a steaming hot mug of coffee.

Cliff is coming by at nine thirty if that's good. He's yours all day."

Van thanked him and started to mention his plan to meet Barbara at ten, but changed his mind. *Better to leave her out of the conversation with Flannery for now.*

The chief gave Van a quick tour of the large condo and showed him where he could shower and shave.

Van wondered why one man needed 3 bedrooms but kept that to himself.

"Now, I've got to get some shut-eye, Van. You can wake me, though if you need anything." He turned and went into the largest bedroom.

By the time Van had undressed, showered, shaved and re-dressed, it was eight forty five. He was quite sure he had time to find something to eat in the big kitchen before Cliff arrived.

After a little searching, he found some cold cereal and a banana. He took an opened carton of milk out of the refrigerator. After a quick sniff he poured it on the cereal. A second cup of coffee heated in the microwave rounded out the meal.

Van tried to make a plan for the day, but his thoughts couldn't progress past meeting Barbara. *That's not going to work. Maybe she's going to be too much of a distraction.*

Come to think of it, he realized she already was one. *But not in a bad way.*

When Cliff showed up, Van was already waiting down in the lobby of the building. He was eager to get started on the investigation.

Cliff shook Van's hand and asked, "Did you get a good sleep in Flannery's mansion?"

Since Cliff brought it up, Van didn't feel too nosy when he asked why the chief had such a large condo.

"Long story short. His ex-wife and two kids lived with him for a short time when he took over as chief but she couldn't stand it here in the city. After a year they split. She took the kids and moved back to the country."

Van wasn't totally surprised. He'd heard plenty of those scenarios. For a few seconds his relationship with Sheila flashed into his mind.

Back on track Van told Cliff of his plan to meet Barbara at City Hall. "Ten o'clock she should be there. Hope you don't mind if she tags along. I think she'll be a help."

Cliff was fine with it but concerned about her safety. "We'll be armed and working legally but she won't be so I'll feel better if she stays in the car when we enter any buildings."

Van agreed. "Of course. Of course. Geez, what was I thinking? Maybe she shouldn't go."

When they got to City Hall and saw Barbara waiting, Cliff parked the car. He and Van got out.

They both let her know their concerns about joining them.

Her response surprised them both. "Oh no, I think it's exciting to be a 'ride along'. That's what they call it, right?"

Chapter 16

Van's borrowed pager vibrated in his breast shirt pocket. Aunt Anna had left a message at the station for him. He was relieved. Chief Rocket had ordered that he not involve her in this part of the case and let him take over at the school. Van was doing that, but he was still worried that she might be in danger.

He and Cliff and Barbara were still standing on the sidewalk in front of City Hall.

"Ah, excuse me guys. My aunt in Baseford called the station. I really need to talk to her." He walked over to a pay phone next to the building away from the buzzing traffic.

Anna sounded worried. She knew she was only supposed to work with Chief Rocket on the murder case, but wasn't used to leaving Van out of things. "I'm sorry, Otto. I don't want to get you in trouble, but I can't figure out how much information to shared with Stan and what isn't worth bothering with. Something happened the other day with Kathleen that I thought you should know about."

Van responded quickly. "That's okay, Anna, but I'm just leaving with another officer to trace some leads. If you can wait until later on today, I might be able to call you from a private phone so you can take all the time you need."

Anna sounded deflated, but Van knew she understood the phone problem. The pager was police issued and could easily be checked.

Someone's personal phone would make it safer for her to share all the details. "That's fine, Otto. And don't worry. Jim and the chief are taking good care of me."

Once Van heard that last comment, he relaxed. *Okay, I feel better now. I know Jim will watch her like a hawk.*

Van ended the call. "Okay, I have to go now. You take care."

"You, too, Love", she said and then he heard the click ending the call at her end.

When Van rejoined Cliff and Barbara, he explained as much about the situation at the boarding school as possible, but concentrated on the murder, itself. He purposely left out the 'Kathleen' angle. Unless Stan Rocket got ahead of him, Van was still determined to straighten that part out himself.

"Okay, let's get to work", he said as he pointed to the idling squad car.

Once they were settled in the warm car he put on a pair of evidence gloves, handed each of them a pair and opened the plastic bag holding the letters. He handed each one a letter. "We'll read these carefully to see if we can find any clues to help identify either the writer or the addressee.

They each read quietly for a few minutes. Barbara found something she thought might be important. "The writer uses the name 'Kay' in this one. Perhaps short for a name like Kathryn?"

Bingo! Or might just be Kathleen. Van had forgotten the girls' last name. He checked the address again. Sullivan. Mrs. Edward. Yes, that was the girls' last name.

At that point, Van decided to fill them in on the mystery girl part of the story.

"What does it say about Kay, Barbara?"

"Well, it looks to me like the writer was worried about her. At one point, she mentioned the girl being very unhappy in the home she had been sent to. Something about a relative not being nice to her."

Van was pleased. Barbara had proved to be a big help in deciphering the letters from a woman's point of view. "I was hoping your insight would pick up something we guys might miss."

He handed her another letter. "This one's postmarked about a week later."

A few minutes went by before she found something. "This might not connect because she doesn't use a name, but it's a young girl, for sure."

Cliff said, "Read it out loud, Barb." She did and both men caught the meaning of the writer's concern. The girl, 'Kay' was possibly not safe with the family taking care of her.

The trio decided to finish reading all of the letters before heading for the address. That exercise didn't produce much, but there was a mention of the town where the family who took her in lived. It was Cornwall, only two towns away from Baseford.

Now that's interesting. But Kathleen had been brought from New York City that day. Supposedly.

* * * * * * * * * *

Barbara sat in the locked squad car, as ordered, across the street from the building Van and Cliff were searching. The return address on the letters was the most obvious start. Van had left the pager with her in case she needed help.

She was only put in charge of reading all the letters again, but Van had made her feel more a part of the case by 'keeping a sharp lookout' for any suspicious activity.

A long dreary hour went by and she was having trouble keeping her eyes open. She didn't sleep, but the leftover warmth of the car made her feel groggy at times. Each time she snapped back to attention, she looked around in all directions. *Oh, Damn. What if I missed something? I don't know how those detectives stay awake on 'stake-outs'.*

The second time she checked all directions, she noticed some motion in the alley across the street. A young boy came out on a bicycle. He looked up and down the street and then rode over to the section of the building that had been the woman's tailor shop. The return address.

The boy got off his bicycle and peered into the shop display window. He kept peering, moving his hand over his eyes to shield the sun.

Barbara grabbed the pen and pad that Cliff had left her and quickly wrote down a description of the boy and his bicycle.

After he tried knocking on the store door a few times, he gave up and left the same way he came through the alley.

Barbara's heart was pounding. *Boy, I didn't know how exciting police work could be.* She hoped that boy would come back soon and find someone in the shop that the guys could question.

A few minutes later, a woman appeared from a door near the edge of the building. She had grey hair and looked to be either late 60's or early 70's. Barbara was flabbergasted when the woman walked right over to the shop door and unlocked it.

She must have bad eyesight if she didn't notice a police cruiser right across the street. Barbara wrote description notes about the woman on the pad, then scrunched down in the seat to watch. It was getting interesting.

No dozing this time. She was on to something important, for sure. Time to call Van.

117

The guys were there in a flash. Just in time to duck behind the car when the boy returned on the bike. This time, the door opened and he walked in.

Cliff opened he car door just enough to whisper to Barbara., "We're going in. This is too convenient to ignore."

Van asked her how she was holding up. "you're in the thick of it, now, girl. Sit tight. If we're not out of there in a half hour, press 9 on the pager and get backup. No, make that fifteen minutes."

She nodded and the guys ran across the street.

Much to their surprise, the door opened when Van knocked. Instead of a sinister scene, they were met with nothing but an elderly woman working at a sewing machine and the boy looking on.

It was obvious they had just interrupted a sewing lesson.

"Goodness me," the woman cried. "You frightened us. What's the problem, officers?" The boy hid behind her. She grabbed his hand. "It's all right, Mario. There must be some mistake."

Van, still not convinced it was all so innocent continued looking around while Cliff got the job of calming the woman and boy down.

"I'm so sorry, Mrs. Um, Capriccio, isn't it? I remember you when you had a tailor shop in here. I used to work for Sam upstairs."

She nodded her head. Ah, Sam. Yes, Sam. He's been gone a long time now. The crazy man left me this building. What's an old lady to do with it?"

She pulled Mario out from behind her. "This is Mario. My grandson. He's wanting to learn to sew, Ah, he makes me proud."

Van joined them and added his own apologies, but quickly asked her if she would help them. "We're trying to solve a murder investigation back in Baseford"

The woman grabbed Mario and covered his ears. Van saw fear in her eyes. "Please, no. Not in front of the boy."

He assured her he would do as she wished. She said simply, "I will be happy to talk with you, but not until the lesson is over and Mario has gone home."

She then took the boy's face in her hands. "Now, Mario, my dear you are not to tell anyone at home about this. Do you understand? "

He nodded, "Yes. Secrets like my lessons, yes Nana?"

She turned back to Van. "It will be fine."

Barbara was counting down the minutes with her finger on the keypad 9 when Cliff came across the street. She breathed a sigh when she saw that he was fine. Not only fine, but laughing. When he got into the car, she demanded to know what was so funny. "I thought I was going to have to call backup and witness a shoot out."

Cliff laughed again. "My God, Barb, I think you watch too much TV."

He supplied the explanation of what had happened and when Van got in, he told them the next plan.

"I'm going to meet her back here tonight. She still lives behind the tailor shop and wants to feed me. What a sweet lady. Pretty neat, huh?"

The looks between Cliff and Barbara did not register amusement.

Van wasn't sure what was wrong. Cliff was quick to let him know of his concern. "I think you've lost some of the NYC caution. How do you know it isn't a setup? I think I should go with you, Van."

Barbara's response was simply, "Yeah, that !!"

Van agreed. Maybe he had become too trusting since moving to sleepy Baseford. It was a plan. They would take a break and Cliff would pick him up at six pm. But where?

Van was faced with his next dilemma. He still had to make the promised call to Anna and hadn't had a chance to ask Barbara if he could use her phone. He hoped she would understand and not be offended.

Barbara looked at Cliff. "What do you think? Should I trust him?"

This time they all laughed. Cliff brought them to Barbara's car. Barbara brought Van to her house to make the call and Cliff was set to pick him up there at 5:45. Van was amazed at how easily that plan fell into place with these two people.

* * * * * * * * * *

"Hi Auntie. Here I am as promised. Using a friend's phone and all ears."

Anna had had a slight run-in with Kathleen the day before and wanted to tell Van before she shared it with Chief Rocket.

"Do you think I should make a big deal out of it or just let it ride and hope it doesn't get worse?"

Van was tempted to hold the story for himself but was more concerned for Anna's safety. He told her to tell Stan every little thing that happened. That girl could be trouble.

Chapter 17

"Kathleen Sullivan, please report to the office." Katy heard the summons over the intercom while she was trying to mix a thick cookie dough by hand in Home Economics class. On a usual school day, she would have been thrilled with the chance to get out of that class. She didn't mind the sewing or even the dull nutrition lessons, but oh, how she hated the mess of cooking.

Today was not a normal school day, though. Katy knew what that call meant. The whole week had been crazy with police snooping all around the school since that horrible man died there.

I know I should feel sorry for him, but I'm not. He deserved to be punished for what he did to me. I knew my uncle would make him suffer.

Katy slammed the big wooden spoon down on the counter with a loud smack. She walked out of the classroom without even a glance at the teacher.

As soon as she stepped out into the long hallway, Katy stopped and looked around to make sure no one was watching. She darted across the hall and into the Girls' Room.

After a quick check into the four toilet stalls, she exclaimed out loud, "Good. No stupid busybodies here"

She pulled at the neckband of her dark green uniform sweater and drew out a gold chain. The links were held together with a small safety pin. Hanging from the chain was a small brass key.

Those lousy cops might try to search me. Ha. I'll give 'em a good show and fight it, she thought. But they won't find anything.

Most of the other girls had already been called in for what they termed 'just routine questioning' concerning what the local rag called 'the recent unfortunate incident'.

Katy mumbled, "Those stupid jerks never tell things like they really are." *They must think we're all a bunch of babies.*

She walked over to the wash stand and looked in the mirror. After trying a few facial expressions, she was ready. "I can play this game. Sad and frightened is what they want to see. I can play this role like a pro."

Katy walked back to the door and counted octagonal gray floor tiles in a line straight from the center of the sill. When she reached the fifth one, she glanced toward the door and listened.

Better put something in front of that door, just in case. The only object available was the large dome topped trash can, hoping it was full and heavy, she hurried to it.

She was in luck. *Good, weird Harold hasn't bothered to empty it yet.*

She dragged it over until it was in line with the outside edge of the door opening. If someone tried to get in, she might hear in time to cover her actions.

Katy repeated her tile count until she got to number seven this time. She bent down and lifted it up. It came up easily. She pulled a plastic sandwich bag from a small hole that had been carved out of the wooden floor underneath.

She quickly dropped the chain and key into the bag and scrunched the bag back into the hole. After replacing the tile, she made sure it was set to the floor pattern correctly and stomped down on it to make sure it was as flat as the rest of the tiles.

Katy was hoping she hadn't taken too much time. She jumped over to the door, pushed the trash can away just enough to squeeze out .

* * * * * * * * * *

Anna was on her way to the kitchen classroom. *What was keeping Kathleen?*

They crashed into each other as Katy dashed out of the girls' room.

Katy apologized. "Oh, I'm so sorry. Umm. I was feeling sick and thought I'd better run into the bathroom first."

Anna put her hand on Katy's head, not really expecting any heat. "Well, you don't look sick to me, young lady."

Katy stammered, "NnnnNo, no. I think I'm all right now."

Anna thought this was a good opportunity to see what was going on in Katy's head. She guided her by the shoulder toward the office. "Do you think you might be nervous because of the police here?"

Katy's face went rigid. After a few seconds, she relaxed again. "No, of course not. But I don't understand why this school is being more protective of us. Why should we be bothered or suffer because of an outside incident?"

Anna certainly hadn't been ready for that. A bone chilling fright wave skittered up her spine but she kept on. "So, you are a little scared, then?"

Katy answered in a mocking sing-song tone. "Oh … Yeah … I'm … real … scared. That's it. HA."

Anna caught the arrogance in Katy's voice. The last thing she wanted to do at that moment was to play detective and continue the confrontation. Otto would expect a full report, though, wouldn't he? She had no choice.

She played the game as if she had sensed nothing. "Oh, dear, Kathleen. I'm sure there's nothing to worry about. The nice officers will just be asking you some simple questions. If you want, I can come in with you."

Anna forced herself to look squarely into Katy's face. The smiled pasted on the thirteen year old freckled face was as fake as a three dollar bill.

Katy returned the stare and barked, "Don't you worry about me, lady. I can take care of myself." She turned away from Anna, chuckled and looked at herself in the huge gilt-edged hallway mirror. "Ever hear of 'street smarts'?

Without giving Anna a chance to reply, she opened the office door and said, "You'd be better off worrying about some of the wimps here."

Anna was taken aback for a moment. *What a fresh girl. So arrogant and full of herself.* She had managed to get Anna angry enough to decide to sit in on the interview after all. Otto would want that.

The more she could find out about this upstart, the better.

Up until that moment there had only been a couple of times Anna was told of her nastiness. So far no one was concerned that it might progress to violence, but now Anna wondered, *Who knows what that girl is capable of?*

Chapter 18

Van was dozing in Barbara's recliner. He thought he heard her voice and a horn beep outside at the same time.

"He's here, Van. Time to go back to work."

He swung his right arm down to the side of the chair, looking for a lever. Barbara laughed as she lowered the chair with a remote control. "We're modern here."

Van patted her on the shoulder as he scooted into the bathroom. "Tell him I'll be right out."

She went to the front door and waved to Cliff. *This must be what it's like to be a policeman's wife.*

Van gave her a little chuck under the chin on his way out the front door. He hoped that would seem gentler than a slap on the back.

* * * * * * * * *

When they got to the building, Cliff offered to go in with Van, but Van felt the woman would feel less threatened if he was alone. "You don't have to stay here for the whole time, but please be back here in two hours. I hope it doesn't take any longer than that."

The lights were on in the shop section and the woman was sewing. He knocked on the door lightly, but the machine whirr must have covered up the sound. He knocked loudly on the window and waved. That worked.

Before he had a chance to ask, she explained that she was working on some samples for Mario's next lesson.

Van apologized for having to bother her with questions and was going to start asking when she stopped him. "No, no. First we eat. Come with me."

Van followed her through a doorway at the back of the shop. She parted two flowered curtains and they were in her immaculate kitchen.

He was amazed at the meal she had prepared in such a short time. First, the aroma hit him like nothing he'd ever smelled before. She hurried around to the stove and started piling heaps of spaghetti onto a plate. "Five or six ?" she asked as she ladled large round meatballs and a rich red gravy onto the pasta.

"Oh my gosh, no. Wait a minute. Just two will be fine."

She shook her head and said, "Never in my kitchen."

Van was faced with five huge meatballs and at least a pound of spaghetti drowned in rich red Italian gravy.

Oh no. I'll never be able to eat all this. What if she won't talk unless I do?

No problem. Talking and eating turned out to be as natural as if he were eating a meal with Aunt Anna. He started by telling how comfortable he felt and about Anna.

He noticed a big smile come over the woman's face. "That is my name, too. Anna Maria Carbone."

Van checked her left hand. She had a sliver of a gold ring on.

He asked as politely as he could if Carbone was her married name.

She chuckled. "No, this full Italian made her whole family furious by marrying an Irishman named Sullivan."

"Wow, that must have made things hard for you."

"At first no one in my family would speak to me, but we were so happy with each other it didn't matter. His family owned a brewery and many bars in New England. He worked for them so we had enough money. And I was very fortunate. They all liked me. Ah, sweet memories."

Van felt sad for her, but had to admit he was secretly tickled that he had possibly found a connection to Kathleen Sullivan.

Van did the best he could. Even though Mrs. Sullivan showed him how to pick up more spaghetti by twirling it into a spoon, he was only able to eat three of the meatballs.

She was disappointed, but seemed satisfied just to watch a young man enjoy her cooking. "Okay, young one. I understand, but you are too skinny. You must eat more."

Van took a breath, wiped his mouth with the dish towel she gave him and relaxed in his chair.

"Now, you have questions for me?"

Ah, finally. Now what to ask first? I've got so many.

Van felt sure it was possible there was a family connection between Anna Marie and Kathleen Sullivan. But how close?

He started by asking her how long ago she was operating the tailor shop. She soon filled in blank spaces and gave him a clear picture of what it was like back then. He found it easy to interject questions about relatives along the way.

Van interrupted her only once when she seemed to drift off into personal memories. "Mrs. S. This is all so helpful, but I have to remind you that I am a detective trying to solve a murder here. I don't want to take advantage of your personal life."

She nodded, then suggested he just ask her definite questions. "I'll try not to reminisce so much. I do tend to ramble."

She got up and went over to her stove. "I almost forgot these."

The tray of anise cookies looked and smelled wonderful.

Van knew what was expected and took two cookies.

I have another cliché for Barbara. They 'melted in his mouth'. The thoughts of Barbara fell softly on him like a floating feather and then were gone.

"Yum", he commented. He wasn't sure if he meant the taste of the cookies or the pleasant fleeting thought of Barbara.

Anna Marie's smile brought him back to the case.

All of a sudden he realized that two hours had passed. Cliff might be back and sitting in his car waiting. Time for only a couple more crucial questions and he had to leave.

Van took a chance and asked the one he had been holding back. "Mrs. S, do you have a young relative named Kathleen?

Her smile faded into a sad, worried look. "Yes, I have a niece by that name. Do you know where she is?"

Van was beginning to trust that Anna, almost as much as his own aunt, but had to be very cautious with information. He managed to at least set her mind at ease when he told her Kathleen was safe. But he couldn't give her any more information.

Anna Marie seemed to understand. "We have a very mixed up family, son. Do you want to come back tomorrow so I can tell you more?"

Yes, he certainly did want to do that. He explained that his driver was waiting. "I really appreciate your cooperation and the meal was fantastic."

He would come back the next day.

"After church, of course and you bring your lady friend."

Lady friend? How did she know he was planning to ask her if that would be okay? He wasn't even sure yet if he would dare to ask Barbara.

"Nine o'clock and I'll make muffins."

* * * * * * * * * *

Cliff started the car as soon as he saw Van coming out of the building. He was anxious to hear what went on. He put his seat belt back on.

Van stopped on the sidewalk right outside the shop. He took the pager out of his pocket and checked it. It was very dark, so Cliff couldn't see Van's face until he came to the car.

Van opened the car door and slid into the passenger seat.

"Sorry, but I need to find another pay phone. Got an important call from another detective on the case."

Cliff nodded and wasted no time finding a phone in front of a well lighted supermarket.

Phil answered right away.

"Hey, Phil. I'm in the city chasing leads. Where are you? What's up?"

Phil was excited. He had some more information about the drunk guy at the bar. He didn't waste time.

"He was there again two nights ago. Name's Frank something. Couldn't squeeze more out of him. He seemed jittery and scared. Looked like he hadn't slept. He asked the bartender if he knew of somewhere he could go hide."

Phil apologized for not getting more info, but promised to go back there that night. "Oh yeah. I snagged a couple of good butts out of the ashtray. Maybe you can use 'em."

"Great, Phil. Thanks. Keep in touch. Okay?"

Van hung up the payphone and followed habit by checking the change tray.

"Home James", he said when he got back into the car. "Not that I know where that is right now."

Once again he had no plans of where to rest his head. Cliff came to the rescue. "Well there's no way we're going to intrude on Barb, so I guess I'm stuck with you this time."

Van was okay with that, but still had to ask Barbara if she would go with him in the morning. "That would be great, Cliff, but I have to ask her something. Do you mind stopping there, first?"

"Okay, okay, but no staying there overnight, ya hear?

The thought hadn't even crossed Van's mind until Cliff brought it up. He wondered why Cliff was so adamant about it.

Barbara was waiting at the front door when they arrived. "What happened? Are you all right? Any trouble? Gosh I was worried."

Cliff hugged her and held her for a minute. "Everything's fine, Sis. Calm down."

Sis? Is that it? If she's his sister, that explains it. Cliff was not just an over protective friend. He was Barbara's brother.

Cliff said to Barbara, "Got a riddle for ya, Barb. When is a date not a date?"

"I don't know, when IS a date not a date?"

Van caught on immediately. He chimed in. "When it's a detective you hardly know asking you to go with him to question an elderly Italian lady !"

They all laughed. Barbara laughed so hard she fell back onto her couch. Van tried to catch her and fell on top of her.

Cliff, still laughing came to the rescue and pulled Van up.

Van put both hands up. "I didn't touch her, officer!"

By the time they settled down, it was decided it would make more sense for them all if they stayed right there at Barbara's house that night. It would save the hassle of driving and pick up times in the morning.

Chapter 19

Van could smell the muffins as soon as he opened the door to the tailor shop. He directed Barbara to the kitchen door.

"I just want to do a last quick check before I go back home."

He didn't expect to find anything. For that matter, he was at a loss for what to look for. It was just a built in detective practice.

Van joined Barb at the door and knocked.

Anna Marie opened it and as soon as they were both in the kitchen, she gave Barbara a big hug.

Van was shocked. By the look on Barbara's face he could tell she was, too. He wondered if she was uncomfortable and would want to leave.

"Hello, Mrs. Sullivan. I'm so happy to meet you." Barb's response was full of friendliness and respect.

Van relaxed. *Whew !! That-a-girl, Barb.*

He knew better than to start firing questions before Mrs. Sullivan served the huge banana muffins and dark espresso.

He had warned Barbara about that rule and she didn't seem the least bit surprised. "Of course. That's just being polite, Van."

He waited for Anna Marie to give the signal. With a chuckle and open arms, she said, "Mangia, mangia. Eat Eat."

She nibbled a few bites and took a cautious sip of the coffee.

Almost on cue to Van's thoughts, she said, "I know you don't have much time so I'll get this started."

Anna had come prepared. Photos of Kathleen were neatly filed in a three ring binder. It was impossible for even Van to not notice that the notebook was covered with a piece of flowered fabric.

"Oh how pretty. Did you cover that, Mrs. S?' Barbara played her part well.

But she sounded genuinely interested, thought Van.

Van tried to follow suit, but was anxious to get his hands on the binder. He reached for it, wanting to grab it, but waited.

Anna Marie handed it over. He opened it to a page near the middle. It was Kathleen, all right. But instead of a scary looking pre-teen, he viewed a pretty little angel in a white dress. It was marked 'confirmation'.

"That's the last one I have of her. It's in chronological order. Look at the beautiful baby on the first page." Anna was beaming.

Van blushed a little. Looking at baby pictures had never been something he was comfortable with but this was an investigation so he conceded.

Kathleen had, indeed been a beautiful baby. So sad she had become an angry young girl. The haunting face came back to him. Anna Marie apologized for the small offering of pictures.

"But is my Kate the girl you were looking for?"

Van nodded and immediately reassured her again that Kathleen was safe.

"I wish I could tell you more. Have you heard from her at all since the date of her confirmation?"

Anna Marie's face grew serious; almost darkened in color. "I wrote many letters to her, but didn't get any back. There was no news even from the few relatives who were still speaking to me. Then one day, about a year later I got a letter. She sounded very unhappy and asked me not to tell anyone anything."

Van found it difficult to curb his enthusiasm. "Do you think she would mind if you shared some of it now?"

"Oh no. If you think it would help. She sounded very afraid, detective. I could tell. And her former sweetness was gone. She was so angry."

Van reached into his shirt pocket. He pulled out two of the letters. "Are these your letters?"

Anna Marie grabbed them and immediately brought them up to nose. She nodded. "Yes, yes. I can still smell my perfume." She began to cry.

Barbara reached over and put her hand on Anna's arm.

Van was surprised at the easy bonding the two women were having. Certainly not something men would do in that situation.

Anna put her head on Barbara's arm and sobbed. There was a noticeable absence of caution and fear.

He was anxious to get past all the uncomfortable emotions and to continue the investigation, but Barbara had already put her other hand on Anna's head and was lightly patting her. He could not interrupt.

So many questions. So little time, he thought. And just when he felt they were getting somewhere.

Van's head was swimming with thoughts and priorities all fighting for first place.

Connect Kathleen to murder.

Aunt Anna's safety.

Barbara.

Phil. Killer's identity.

Barbara.

Gina. Search results in Baseford.

Barbara.

Each time he thought of Barbara he was touched by the scene in front of him. *Two women who don't even know each other can understand and console with no walls, no rules, no games. How can they do that?*

Van wondered why men couldn't do that. But he knew there was no answer. It was just the way it was and he couldn't change it. Humans all have their own skills and talents; their own make-up passed on from generation to generation. It all has to do with the genes.

Barbara broke into his thoughts. "Van. Mrs. S is ready to talk with you again."

Click … click … Van switched from philosopher to detective.

"Oh, thank you. I'm so sorry to put you through this, but it's really necessary. You're helping me a lot."

Van let Anna Marie hold the two letters while he asked questions, but he was hoping she would voluntarily put them down on the table before he would have to take them back.

More remembered details of Anna Marie's letter to Kathleen convinced Van that something very traumatic had happened to her.

Anna remarked, "The few times she did write back, she used words like, horrible, disgusting, shocking, frightening. What concerned me most was her last words. She said it was embarrassing and she was terribly hurt. It ended with what felt like pure anger to me. Did someone do her harm?"

Van had to admit it sure sounded that way. The look on Kathleen's face that night could have been one of revengeful satisfaction. Was the dead man the one who hurt her?

Anna Marie repeated her question. "Did someone hurt my Kate?"

Van explained that it sounded like it to him. He shared as much as possible with her about the girl's recent attitude, but tried to soften it.

"She must have a lot to deal with and work out right now."

Anna gave the letters back and asked again about where Kathleen was. Van assured her the girl was safe, though he, himself was harboring doubts.

Time to leave Mrs. Sullivan before her safety might be compromised and time to get back home.

Van and Barbara left the kitchen with a paper bag holding four muffins and a plastic container of cream cheese.

Anna Marie walked with them to the tailor shop front door..

She gave them both hugs before they left.

"I hope to see you young people again."

Chapter 20

The drive back to Barbara's house was full of chatty conversation. Barbara was paying attention to driving her Toyota Corolla but was still full of questions and Van was busy trying to decide how much to tell her before he answered each time.

"This is hard for me," he said. "It's so easy to talk to you, but I have to keep some things to myself."

She reassured him. "I know this is work for you. This was all part of a murder investigation, not just a fun breakfast visit."

Van ended up sharing a little about the appearance of Kathleen Sullivan at the school, but no details about her attitude or possible connection to the murder.

Barbara started to giggle.

Van was curious about what was so funny.

Barbara gulped down a couple of chuckles. "I was just thinking about Cliff's reaction to you staying at my house. He said he only gives his permission for you to stay at my house tonight because he knows you won't have made any plans on your own."

Van's response was a loud laugh. "Hah. Once again he's right. It didn't take him long to figure me out. But is that all right with you? I mean the staying overnight?"

Barbara agreed, then added, "It seems like all three of us are quite comfortable with each other, doesn't it, Van?"

Van nodded, but he was puzzled about Cliff giving him permission to be with Barbara. He asked her if she thought he should check in with Cliff when they got to her house.

Barbara solved that problem for him. " No worries, Van. It's his day off and he's at my house waiting for us."

Perfect timing with these two. I get the feeling I'm not running this show. But it's not a bad feeling. I'll just go with it.

When they got to Barbara's house, Cliff was up on a ladder cleaning out gutters. Barbara explained. "I've got a leak somewhere on that corner of the house."

She waved at Cliff, using the hand holding the bag of muffins. "I'll heat these up."

Once inside the house, she guided Van to the living room couch and said, "Rest, think, collect thoughts, make plans, whatever you have to do next. Real coffee coming up."

Van started to ask for some paper and a pen, but she was already tossing them to him.

He leaned his head against the back of the couch. *Just need to relax a minute.*

The next thing he knew, he woke up to a cup of hot coffee on the coffee table very close to his face. He had fallen over on the couch and sleep had grabbed him.

He sat up and saw Cliff sitting in a chair across from him. Barbara was serving the heated muffins.

"Sorry to bother you, buddy, but I have plans tonight so I'll be leaving soon. Anything you want to tell me?"

It took a few minutes for Van to clear his fuzzy head. The coffee helped. Barbara offered to leave the room so the policemen could be comfortable.

Van shook his head. "No, no. You stay. Your take on this morning might help."

Van had to lead in but the whole session ran like clockwork.

Cliff's questions. Van's answers, Barbara's perspective circled the room in a sure, but casual way. He marveled at the ease of their interactions.

Cliff ended it. "Well, I don't know if we've helped any, but it sure was a pleasure working with you, Van."

Van reminded him that think tanks didn't often produce instant results, but they almost always helped. He thought of his aunt and repeated her theory of looking for a catch. "Sometimes the piece to hold everything together can be hard to recognize. Maybe you'll think of something."

Van told them he was planning to go back to Baseford in the morning. Cliff wouldn't be free to bring him to the train station, but Barbara could do that on her way to work.

Van shook Cliff's hand when he left the house. "It's been a pleasure to meet you, Cliff. And an added pleasure to have your help. I hope we meet again."

Cliff reached forward and gave him a sideways man hug. "Same here, Van."

"Don't you two do anything I wouldn't do now."

Barbara and Van got a good long laugh about that order.

Needless to say the evening passed quite coolly. The closest they got to each other was watching a couple of sci-fi movies on the couch. Each at their respectful end. They both started heavy yawning back and forth after the second movie.

Barbara set Van up again in the recliner and she disappeared to the back of the house somewhere. Van was curious, but too tired to think long about it.

* * * * * * * * * *

The next morning, Barbara tried to make him feel comfortable. Clean towels were on the coffee table. "I know you know your way around the bathroom already. I have my own, so don't worry about me."

Soon they were in her car and headed to the train station. Van was getting hungry. "Don't you eat breakfast in the morning?"

"Nope. There's a great little food truck that parks in the city lot every morning. No work, no dishes for me."

I like this. I like it a lot. Van was finding more and more he liked about her. Maybe he should tell her?

They came to the station quickly. Too quickly for Van's thinking.

Barbara offered to wait with him for a little while. "Plenty of time before I have to be at work."

They found a seat inside the station and sat for a while. Van's thoughts were racing. He realized he might never get to see her again.

"Um, we can exchange phone numbers if you want. Just in case you get some ideas about the … oh crap" He reached over and kissed her.

She kissed him back.

The next kiss was wrapped in a hug.

Chapter 21

S tan dreaded making the call. "So sorry to have to bother you, Anna."

She sounded groggy so he guessed she had been asleep.

"Oh, Stan. It's no bother. What's wrong?"

He apologized again for waking her so late at night, then explained. He didn't want to worry her, but they had picked Kathleen up out on the main road.

"She's fine. Not hurt or anything. But you should come down to the station soon if you can. I can have Kevin pick you up if you want."

He apologized again. They couldn't find anyone else and the girl was not helping.

Anna's response was quick. "I'll be there in half an hour."

That surprised him. Before he could measure his words he asked, "Really?" He hoped he hadn't offended her.

She sounded wide awake when she answered. "Of course. Yes, Stan. It's clear you don't know me very well."

That was true. But he was liking what he had found so far.

* * * * * * * * * *

Janice was frantic. She didn't know what to do. Frank Gambrel had just stormed out of her apartment. The only thing she could think of was to call Phil. Even if he got mad he might help.

She dialed his number. *Please God let him be there. Pleases make him listen.*

Phil answered. He cleared his throat, then yelled, "This better be important, Babe."

"Oh my God, Phil. You gotta help me. This is serious." She started to cry.

Phil's voice softened. "Okay, Honey. I'm here. What's the matter?"

"Frank Gambrel was here. I was so scared. He says he's going to kill himself."

Phil told her she had done the right thing to call him. "It's going to be all right. Just tell me everything."

Janice choked down a couple of tears and began. "I thought it was my sister at the door. You know how she knocks really hard. Oh God."

Frank had barged in as soon as she opened the door and told her to shut it. As soon as she did, he locked it.

At first she was afraid, but she and Frank had been friends since high school so that wore off quickly. She could see he was the one filled with fear. He was in trouble.

"He was a mess. Shaking all over and his eyes were glassy. I know he was into drugs lately. Pretty heavy."

Phil stopped her. "You didn't give him any money, did you?

Janice felt anger rising. A twinge of the old problems between them.

Phil must have realized the same. "I'm sorry, Babe. Stupid question."

She continued. Frank told her he couldn't stand the guilt anymore. It was killing him, so he might as well be dead.

"Jesus, Phil. He told me he's the one who murdered that guy Van found at the school. That was when I started to be afraid he would kill me, too."

She started to sob.

Phil tried to calm her down. He would come over there if she wanted.

"Okay, Hon. I'll be there soon. I'll knock our usual knock. Take it easy, now."

Janice was relieved. He believed her. He was worried about her, too.

Phil said he was going to call Van first but he would hurry.

* * * * * * * * * *

Anna rushed into the station. Stan jumped out of his chair to go meet her.

"I got here as fast as I could, Stan. What happened?"

He guided her into his office and closed the door. He pointed to one chair and sat down in another right next to it.

"Well, I don't know how to make this easy or say it nicely, but we caught Kathleen in a sting set up. She was trying to buy cocaine."

Anna was shocked. She found it hard to believe that a fourteen year old girl could even know how to do that. But she had to admit that there wasn't much about Kathleen that fit a young girl of that age.

"I feel rather stupid and naïve, Stan. It's hard to understand. Are you sure someone didn't set her up? She's managed to alienate almost all of my girls."

Stan shook his head. Not only had Kathleen made the connection herself but she admitted it and was angry that she hadn't scored.

"I'm sure this must be hard for you to fathom. To be honest it's something I've never had to deal with either."

Stan went on to explain that because Kathleen was a juvenile they could not keep her at the jail more than six hours. He hoped that Anna would take her back to the school. "Otherwise we'll have to let her go free or call in the state agency to pick her up."

Anna sighed. She had no clue how to handle the situation.

"I guess I don't have a choice, then. I can't find any family contacts, either, so I'll have to figure something out . Looks like I've got me a wayward daughter, Stan."

Stan looked a bit relieved, but she could tell he was still very concerned. He offered to have officer Flood follow her home if that would help.

"Do you think she would try to run away?"

He doubted that, but shared his personal feelings about Kathleen's brave attitude.

"I'm no expert, but I think there's a scared little girl under all that."

* * * * * * * * *

Two loud knocks and three in a row. Their old private signal. Janice opened the door just a crack, leaning her full weight against it.

It was Phil. She opened it wide and fell into his arms.

"It's okay, Babe. I gotcha. Van is on his way."

He didn't try to pull away, just moved enough to kick the door closed behind him.

Janice let herself relax a little in the embrace, but soon the reality of the situation took over.

She whispered, "What if he comes back? W-what if he does kill himself? W-will Van be mad if he can't get a confession?" What if ... "

Phil released the hug and grabbed her arms. He tried to quiet her but all he could do was hold tight and shake his head.

She finally clamped her mouth shut and took a couple of deep breaths. She shook his hands off her arms. "I'm fine now. Honest. I should probably try to write it all down before Van gets here."

Janice went to her desk to get paper and a pen.

Phil locked the door then stood watch at the window overlooking the stairs leading up to the apartment.

* * * * * * * * * *

Anna sat on one of the hard chairs in the interrogation room. Kathleen sat across from her. No one was with them, but Stan was watching and listening on the other side of the one way window.

Anna was trying to ignore the ferocious face Kathleen was putting on.

Try to think of her as Stan said. A frightened little girl.

Easy to say, but not so easy to do and what should she say? The word frightened came back to her. Anna had an idea.

"Kathleen, I want you to know this whole thing frightens me.. I want to help you, but I'm afraid I don't know how to do it right."

Kathleen didn't respond, but Anna noticed a slight relaxing of the girl's facial muscles.

Anna worried. Had she messed it up already? Would Kathleen's next act be her sinister smile and sneering laugh?

Well, she didn't have much time, so she decided to dive bravely into threatening mode. "Kathleen if we can't make any headway here, the chief will have to call the state agency. They will take you somewhere and keep you until they find the people responsible for you. Is that what you want?"

The stone face turned into a pout. Anna had at least made her think.

"What the hell are you afraid of, you witch? I'm the one in trouble. You've got a great life."

Anna saw the girl's lips begin to tremble. A glimmer of hope crept in.

Keep going. Just keep going.

"I told you. I'm afraid I won't be able to help you. I've never had to face that possibility before. I've always been in control and been the one to fix my girls' problems. Always making things better."

Kathleen started to laugh. A slow chuckle and then a full 'hah' came out.

Anna lowered her head. She thought she had failed for sure, but then she heard a soft sob.

Kathleen had caved in. She was rocking back and forth on the chair and hugging herself. She was trying to gulp back each sob.

"It's okay, dear. It's okay. Go ahead. Let it all out."

Anna started to cry, too.

* * * * * * * * * *

By the time Van got to Janice's apartment, she had calmed down. She and Phil were sitting next to each other on her couch. He had helped her write everything down, by asking what she called typical detective questions here and there.

She noticed and was happy that he kept it serious and didn't ask any more stupid questions about her money.

Van was now the one asking the questions.

"Did he tell you why he killed the guy?"

Janice looked at the notes. "Yes. It sounds freaky to me, but he said he owed Kathleen's grandfather a lot of money and even though the old man was in jail for life he got guys to find Frank."

She stopped. Van persisted. "Is that all?"

"No," she continued, "He said they were going to kill him if he didn't get rid of the guy who had raped the girl's mother."

"Wow !" That's amazing, Jan. But it was a particularly brutal murder. Did he say anything more about that?"

"Yes, that was what he felt the most guilty about. The men were with him when he killed the guy and they forced him to do something awful to him. He wouldn't say what and I don't think I want to know."

Van agreed. "you're probably right about that."

She didn't know what he was driving at the time, but Janice remembered that Frank's ex-wife owned a small cabin on Tarpon Lake near there.

Van clapped his hands. "Great. I bet he's holed up there."

He used Janice's phone to wake Jim up at home.

After a few cracks about Van being a slave driver, Jim got excited, too. Not only did he know Frank, but he also knew where the cabin was.

"Ginny and I went out there for a couple of cookouts back when Frank was married. Can you hang out for ten to fifteen minutes? I can bring you there."

Chapter 22

"Oh, Mrs. Gorham, I don't know what to do," Kathleen sobbed as she dabbed her tears with the handkerchief Anna had given her.

Anna's face was lined with tears, too. Kathleen was sorry to have made her cry. Sorry for everything all at once. It was like a heavy rock of sorrow around her neck and she didn't know what to do with it.

Anna asked if she might feel better after she told her story. "And it would help the police to close the case."

Yes, yes. I do need help. This whole thing has turned into such a mess.

"All right. And you can bring the chief in. I might as well tell him, too."

When Stan came in the interrogation room he brought hot tea for Anna and a cola for Kathleen. "Sorry, kid. We don't have the real stuff here."

"We could move to my office if you would like. The chairs are more comfortable."

Kathleen liked that idea. The room was not making her feel at ease. "Okay. I feel like I'm a criminal in here."

155

Once they were seated in the office, Stan told them that Van was back from New York City.

The mention of New York City surprised Kathleen. "Oh God, what about the city?"

"Nothing to worry about. Van is one of my detectives. He went there to follow up on some leads. Anna, why don't you explain your connection to him?"

Anna did a quick as possible family connection story so Stan could continue.

"So, you see, we have found your aunt Anna Marie and the letters she wrote to your mother. Can you tell us anything else about them?"

Kathleen took a deep breath, let out two more sobs and said, "Okay, okay. Looks like I don't have a choice now. What do you want to know?"

Stan had a list of questions ready. First … They had identified the victim but wondered if the murder was connected to Kathleen's secret arrival at Harrinton House.

She started to cry again. *Please, please don't make me talk about it. It hurts so bad.*

Stan tried to console her. "It looks like this whole mess has been causing you a lot of personal pain. I'm sorry for that, Kathleen."

She was quiet for a few minutes, then decided to trust them.

But she was worried. "Am I in any trouble, myself, here?"

Both Stan and Anna assured her she was not. Anna added, "Everything is okay at the school and I know Stan is doing everything possible to protect you."

Kathleen couldn't hold back any longer. She blurted out, "He was a terrible man !! My mom's boyfriend."

She jumped out of the chair. "He … he beat her up and raped her !!"

She began pacing back and forth. "I'm GLAD he's dead !!"

Kathleen glared at Stan. "What else do you want?. What else?"

Anna patted the cushion on the chair Kathleen had been sitting in.

"It's okay to be angry. I would be, too. C'mon. Sit down."

Stan didn't say anything until Anna had diffused some of Kathleen's anger and convinced her to sit down again.

Anna asked the next question. "Do you think they brought you to my school to protect you from him, maybe?"

"That's another thing that makes me mad. Nobody told me anything. My grandfather gives all the orders from a jail cell out in Texas and we all have to follow them."

She eventually calmed down enough to see that she would be safer there than anywhere else. "I have to admit, I was afraid of him, that's for sure."

Once the chief had answers to almost everything on his list, he went over to his file cabinet and pulled out the bundle of letters. "These were found in a local airport locker. They were written by your aunt Anna Marie Sullivan to your mother. What can you tell us about them?"

The sight of the letters made Kathleen's heart beat faster. She had questions of her own. "Is my aunt all right? Where is Mario? And Colleen….how is she?"

The chief's phone rang. Van gave Stan a quick rundown of the scene at Janice's apartment. "Jim is on his way to pick us up with his jeep. He knows where the cabin is. We're hoping to find Frank before he tries to kill himself."

"Great Van … Okay. Let me know if you need backup."

Stan had a hard time controlling his excitement, but took a deep breath, sent a knowing glance to Anna and focused on Kathleen.

"Van won't be able to come to the station after all. Sorry, but he's busy chasing down some new leads in the case."

"He's the detective who went to the city, right?"

Stan answered, "Yes and once he was here, we thought you might like him to try to call your aunt?"

Kathleen gasped. "Oh my God. You would do that? Is it safe?"

Stan nodded, then told her he had the number and could make the call himself.

She didn't give him a chance to say more. "Can we do it now?"

Chapter 23

The road into the woods to the cabin was obviously seldom used. Janice was not happy to be there, but Van asserted his legal authority and made it a formal request.

"We need you there in case Frank is still alive, Janice. You know him better than we do and he's already reached out to you once. You might be able to talk him out of it. Phil, I need you to stay here in case he comes back."

She braced herself by hanging on to a flimsy leather strap attached to the roof of Jim's jeep. It wasn't her imagination that the twists, turns and crashes into washed out holes made it uncomfortable. The only one not complaining was Jim who could see it all coming as he drove along.

At one point he came to a complete stop and had she and Van get out and walk on higher ground while he drove through water that reached the tops of his tires.

When they got back in, he told them he was pretty sure that a vehicle had recently gone through there. "The tracks coming out of that spot were deep and new since the last rain. The cabin isn't far from here and my guess is our man is there."

Janice winced. "I hope the rest of the ride is smoother."

Van added, "And I hope he's alive."

"And I hope he's written a confession if he isn't", Jim said as he pulled forward onto smoother ground. "There you go, Jan. Should be better now."

After a couple of long curves, one to the left and one to the right they came to a stand of pine trees. The end of the road, for sure, and where they had to leave the jeep.

"But where is his car?" Van asked.

Jim pointed to the right where a single space was carved out of the trees. It was there. The old jalopy that Frank managed to keep for himself after the divorce. "He's here. Hard to believe that junker is still running."

"Okay, Jimbo, what's next?"

Jim cautioned them. "It's a fairly steep walk from here to the cabin, so be careful. I'll go first, then Van, then Janice."

Janice's voice came out in a squeak. "How far?"

"Maybe 20 to 30 feet but it's downhill and the cabin is right at the bottom. Van, when we get there I'll circle around to the front door. You can watch through the kitchen window straight to the front."

"Okay, Boss." It was a grab at levity. They both knew how to take turns at "leader" when necessary. "Thank God we have some daylight left."

Please let him be alive so I can witness his confession. Van knew from experience that it wasn't often that simple. *Okay, a note will do. Frank had already told Janice that he was the killer. That would probably be enough.*

They came upon the cabin so abruptly that Janice bumped into Van's back and fell backwards. He helped her up as quietly as possible, but reminded her to be silent. He prayed they hadn't already made too much noise.

Jim was at the front door in a flash. Van watched him walk in and look around. He motioned for Van to go in and pointed to the back door. It wasn't locked so he opened it.

Jim met them there. "It's over. He did it. No mess, so Jan can come in, too."

The scene was indeed not messy. The Beretta 9 millimeter pistol was on the kitchen table next to a signed confession. Frank's body was leaned back on the couch looking like he had totally relaxed with his last breath. A rubber tube was still tied tightly on his left arm.

On the coffee table was a syringe and 4 empty packages that smelled like heroin.

The suicide note, also signed was on the coffee table.

"I can't live with it anymore. I didn't want to kill him, but I owed the old man too much money.

I didn't know I would have to cut him.
Oh God I didn't want to. but I was afraid
they would kill me if I didn't.
It doesn't matter anymore. I'm so sorry."

"Janice, was he right or left handed?"

"Ummm, pretty sure it was right. Ahh, is it okay if I sit in this chair?"

"Oh my gosh," Jim said. "I forgot you were with us. Sorry"

Van took her arm and led her to an upholstered chair on the opposite side of the room. "So sorry, Janice. Are you all right? Need some water?"

Jim interrupted. "Don't think the water would be turned on, Van. But the lake water is very clean if you want me to get some."

Janice shook her head. "No, no. I'm all right now. Umm, Van, why did you ask me about Frank's hand?"

Van explained. He was making sure that he would be able to give himself the lethal injection. "Just convincing myself that someone else didn't do it to him."

Jim read the suicide note out loud.

"I don't think someone else would let him mention the boss in prison, do you? That's pretty incriminating. We know who that is, right?"

Van agreed, but said he was hoping Frank had written the grandfather's name somewhere.

"Ahh, guys," Janice said faintly. "He told me his name and I wrote it down in my notes before you came over, Van."

She stood up and started pacing back and forth. "Oh damn, does that mean I'll have to go to court?"

Van couldn't answer that question. He had no idea how the whole case would turn out. He just shook his head. "I hope not, Janice."

Jim joined her pacing for a few steps and put an arm around her. She calmed a little but started to cry. Not a hard cry, but more one of resignation. "What a mess."

Van went to work. He asked Jim where he could find plastic bags in the kitchen. The regular kind would not be best, but he had been in a rush to get to Janice's apartment and didn't bring any gloves or evidence bags with him.

Jim helped Janice back into the chair, making sure she was more calm.

He started to go to the kitchen for anything suitable, but stopped.

"Hey, boss. Can't we just wait for the ambulance team and forensics to do this?"

Van had just come to that same conclusion. "Duhhh. Exactly what I was just thinking. I'll call the ambulance and Gina. When I get the chief, you need to give him directions to get here."

Janice chuckled, softly. "Quite the dynamic duo. Now what about Phil?"

Chapter 24

C hief Rocket was pleased with the outcome of his call to Anna Marie in New York City. He connected right away and watched as Kathleen slowly morphed into a totally different young girl while talking with her aunt. He and Anna exchanged puzzled glances.

I wonder if she notices the big change, too. It's so huge that I am already having trouble recalling the nasty, mean attitude Kathleen initially brought with her.

The station phone on his desk rang. It was quickly answered by one of the officers out in the main section. Stan could see what was going on. Kevin signaled to him to take the call out there. He mouthed "VAN".

"Sorry. I have to go, but she can take a few minutes more while I'm gone. Anna, are you okay with this?"

Anna nodded. "Sure, Stan. Sure. No problem."

He put his hand on her shoulder as he passed her chair. "You are what my mom would call a 'brick', Anna. And that's an all good thing."

Once Stan was out of earshot from the office, he grabbed the phone.

"Yeah, Van. What's up?"

Within a couple of minutes, Stan was yelling out orders. "Two cars, four guys, no sirens. Kevin with me. Follow us. I have directions. You drive, Kev."

Anna could see the activity happening from Stan's office. She told Kathleen to end her call. "We'll call again, soon, Kathleen. I promise."

Stan walked toward his office, but Anna waved him away. He could tell the call was over. Both Anna and Kathleen were gathering their things, getting ready to leave.

* * * * * * * * * *

The ride back to the school was still heavy with tension. Kathleen was not convinced she wasn't going to be charged with some kind of felony. Anna wasn't too sure of that, herself, but she tried to console her.

"I'm just guessing, but I don't think they would let you go home if Stan intended to do that."

By the time Kathleen got out of Anna's car at Harrington House, she had explained her secrecy about the broken chain and locker key she had hidden in the bathroom floor and was ready to show Anna.

"The guys brought me here so fast I didn't have time to connect with mom. She told me not to give it to anyone else, especially them, so I hid it."

Anna was quite surprised at the girls' ingenuity. "Great idea. How did you come up with that?"

Kathleen laughed. Oh, I saw it done on a TV show once. Only that one they didn't find until years later when they tore the building down."

Anna sighed. I'm glad this mystery is closer to being solved right now.

* * * * * * * * * *

By the time Stan and his men got to the cabin, Gina and her team were already there. She met him at the squad car as soon as he got out.

"Van was correct. I hate to admit that. The poor bastard mainlined himself with more heroin than the worst addicts would dare use. He must have known every dealer in the area to find it all."

Stan just nodded sadly. He knew Frank Gambrel's reputation and habits. He had been able to make a couple of dealer arrests just by following Frank around in the past.

"Thanks, Gina. No loss to society, but still sad. I never get used to it."

She shook her head. "Nope, never."

Van joined them. "Okay to let the ambulance take him, Gina?" Chief, do you want to see him first?"

Gina gave Stan a few minutes to answer, 'no' then gave Van the go-ahead. "By the way, Van, good call on C.O.D.. I'll wrap up my work here and get my guys out soon, Chief."

Stan felt a little like a bump on a log. But thankful he had such a good team. *I must have the best group of people in the world here. Nothing for me to do but go back to my office and wait for all the reports to hit my desk.*

Then reality hit him. "Just so I know what's going on now, where are Jim and Janice? And Phil? I'll need to talk to them ASAP, Van."

"Jim drove Janice back to her apartment and Phil is there still." Jan wrote a pretty thorough report for me, so I'm sure she will be a big help, Chief."

Chapter 25

It was a glorious Spring Day. The temperature was expected to rise up into the low 70's by early afternoon. Jim's wife, Ginny's station wagon was packed with balloons and gaily wrapped gifts of all sizes. She and Van's New York City friend, Barbara were on their way to the White Horse Inn.

Barbara pushed a few balloons toward the back seat and asked, "Can you believe all that has happened in the past few months?"

Ginny shook her head. "It's mind boggling even for me and I really wasn't that involved. Would you have believed back then that your life would change so quickly?"

Barbara answered, "Never. I hope I can do a good job at the school. And I pray everyone has the patience to bear with me while I learn from the expert."

"OH, Barb. Don't be silly. Mrs. Gorham would never have suggested you for her replacement if she didn't have full confidence in you. That was her baby."

Ginny was completely enjoying her new vocation. She was in charge and had planned every aspect of the celebration.

Underneath her concerns, Barbara was delighted with the recent changes in her life.

The two women continued their surprise laced conversation back and forth until they reached the inn parking lot.

Ginny parked her car in front of the entrance. "You wait here while I go get a cart or something to put all this in or on."

Barbara welcomed another chance to be alone. To think and enjoy the prelude to a new life.

* * * * * * * * * *

Van heard the horn honking out in front of his apartment, but didn't bother to hurry. Jim was early and Van took advantage of that. This was going to be a very busy special day and he was not on duty for a change. After a few minutes, Jim figured that out. He shut the car off and used his key to let himself in.

"Knock, knock. Coming in, ready or not."

Van came nonchalantly out of the bathroom. "You are way too early, Jimbo. Did Ginny kick you out cuz you were getting in the way?"

"No, she left a long time ago with all the presents and supplies. She only needed me to help load up."

Van pulled 3 shirts out of his closet and asked Jim which one would go best with the slacks he had on. Jim declined to make the choice. "No way, man. I'm not going to be the blame if Barbara doesn't approve."

They both knew better. "Barb would never say anything even if she didn't like it, Jim."

Van closed his eyes, put on one shirt and tossed the others onto the bed. "Let's change the subject. How are you doing now that Ginny has her own catering business?"

Jim was enthusiastic. "Great. Really great. She was always good at organizing things anyway and we all know what a good cook she is."

Van quizzed Jim more. "I mean how are you doing with her being so busy?"

Jim's answer was simple. "I feel better now when I have long shift hours, so it's good for both of us."

Van clapped him on the back and said, "Okay buddy. Ready to roll."

* * * * * * * * * *

Anna stood alone out in the front circular drive at the school. She was still in her pajamas and bathrobe. The same things she had been wearing the night of the murder. She was alternately melancholy, then happily relieved. In just one week, she would be training Barbara Cronin to take over as the manager of Harrington School. And training herself to let go of the reins she had been holding for many years. Anna was surprised that Barbara was willing. And also surprised that she and Van had not jumped right into a romantic relationship. *Young people nowadays. Can't understand them.*

Kathleen burst through the front door. "Anna, Anna. You're going to be late. Come and get dressed !!"

"Yes, Dear. I'm coming. Can't keep that beautiful dress your aunt made waiting, can I?"

Anna noticed that Kathleen was already dressed in a pretty pink dress. *Not the same girl who came here a few months ago. She smiled and gave her a hug.*

* * * * * * * * * *

The parking lot at the White Horse Inn was filling up. Ginny and Barbara were surveying their work. "It's lovely, Ginny. They will all want to be your next clients."

"Well, the proof will be the goodies. But that's the area I'm most comfortable in, anyway."

A small group of people ambled over to where they were standing. Barbara recognized one of them right away. It was Anna Marie, Kathleen's aunt from New York City.

"Hello, girls. What a wonderful job you've done here, Mrs. Barone."

I'd like you to meet Kathleen's mother, Doris Sullivan."

A young girl was standing close behind Doris. She stepped out and introduced herself. "And I'm her cousin, Colleen. Pleased to meet you."

Doris spoke next to Barbara. "I'm so glad to meet the woman who helped the detectives untangle our mess."

Barbara blushed and insisted she didn't do much to help.

"Nonsense!", said Anna Marie. "It was you who made me feel comfortable enough to speak up."

"By the way, where are those brave men?"

Anna Marie took Barbara's arm and pulled her off to the side. "What's happening with you and that young man? I thought you would be married by now."

Barbara blushed again. She shook her head. "We're okay. Just taking it slow. I will be totally immersed in the school and he still has things to work out with his Sheila."

Just then Van and Jim came through the banquet hall door. And right behind them came Phil and Janice, arm in arm.

"Guess things are patched up between them, now?", whispered Ginny with a giggle.

* * * * * * * * * *

Van looked around for familiar faces. He found Barbara's first. *Geez. Why does that always happen?*

The group surrounding her became familiar one by one after that. He was glad they had all found each other. But where was aunt Anna? Kathleen had taken over the job of getting her there. He wondered if he should call Anna, but remembered how tickled Kathleen had been when she was given that responsibility.

Van didn't know a lot of the guests, so he was relieved and even happy to see Gina Taylor come through the door. Behind her was one of the station officers. It was Kevin, the one who had helped him the night of the murder. Piling in right behind them was a group of officers from Baseford. From then on the door stayed open as many more people poured in that Van did not know.

My aunt has lived here for a long time, so she probably knows everyone.

Speaking of her, he wondered again. Where was she?

Just as he was about to use the wall phone to call, he heard the sound of horses' hoofs on the pavement outside.

Others heard it, too. They all stopped talking and went to look out the windows and door.

The sight was something no one expected.

An open white buggy festooned with flowers of every color Ginny could find was coming to a halt. Oohs and ahhs floated around the room.

The driver, with great ceremony, got out and helped Kathleen down.

Next, he assisted Anna. Anna was dressed in a beautiful blue satin dress and holding a bouquet of flowers matching the collection from the buggy.

Her silver hair was braided and circled on top of her head. A simple white flower sat on top.

The driver tried to help the next passenger out, but was waved off. Out stepped Stan Rocket.

There was a complete crowd intake of breaths. No one who knew Stan had ever seen him dressed up. Not even a regular suit.

He looked like a movie star. His snow white hair matched the lapels of his light blue suit. He was beaming !!

Kathleen stepped in front of them and linked Anna's arm through Stan's. Another beaming face led the couple into the banquet hall.

The piano player started. Everyone sang. "Here comes the bride."

Much later, after the gifts had been opened and Ginny's cake demolished, Van sat with Anna and Stan.

They watched Kathleen proudly showing off her repaired gold chain with her mother's cross on it. She came over to Van. "Thank you for finding the catch in our broken family. This chain will always be my reminder that you brought us all together safely." She teared up, gulped it back and gave Van a hug before running off to her own relatives.

Van was impressed. "Well, isn't that something? That young lady has come full circle, hasn't she?"

They nodded in agreement, then fell into a comfortable silence.

Van broke it with a question for Stan. "Do you really think I've got what it takes to fill your shoes?"

Stan put an arm around Van. "It's all yours, Van. When we get back from our trip, I'll be there for you. But I know you can handle it."

Van looked him in the eye. "I'm honored, Sir."

Acknowledgements

Many thanks to all who helped me accomplish this feat.

I certainly could not have done it without you.

Especially to:

Andrew Gorman
Leanne Campbell
Mary Montanaro
Jan Rupert

And everyone else who took the time to read, listen and comment.